Lockwood kept up the lecture the entire way back to the Phoenix. Matt tried to tune him out. He got the gist of it: Matt was a terrible, selfish person who should just smile and accept that he was stuck here.

It's not fair, Matt thought.

They finally got to the hotel. Before Matt could get out of the car, Lockwood put a hand on his shoulder. "You need to think about what I'm saying, Matt. What you're doing here matters. You can glorify God, or bring reproach on His name. It's up to you."

Matt said nothing, pulling away from the older man. He was starving. He hoped there was still something to eat in the dining room.

His father was waiting for him in the doorway of the dining room. "Matt!" What happened?"

"I just took a walk," Matt said as he tried to go by.

His father grabbed his arm. "Matt, listen to me. Your bad attitude is obvious to everyone here. You know better than this. You need to change your outlook."

That did it.

Matt had already suffered a lecture from Lockwood for the past half hour. His dad starting in on him was the straw that broke the camel's back.

He pulled away from his father. "Look, I didn't want to come here! You and Mom made me! I hate this stinking country, and I hate you!"

Bile in his throat, Matt turned on his heel and stomped off to his room, his anger overpowering his appetite.

Other books by Laura Ware

Dead Hypocrites

The Silent Witness

Redemption

TWO WEEKS
IN
GUYANA

LAURA WARE

TWO WEEKS IN GUYANA

JJ Press
www.jjpressflorida.com

To my brothers and sisters in Guyana, South America. May God continue to bless you as you serve Him and spread His word.

ACKNOWLEDGEMENTS

As always, this book came about thanks to the help of a number of people.

First and foremost, I must give thanks to God for the opportunities He's given me to travel to another land to spread His word.

I've had the opportunity to visit the country of Guyana several times, twice on medical mission trips. I'd like to thank the group of Christians whom I was privileged to serve with on medical mission trips in 2005 and 2006.

Steve DeLoach, who lives part-time in Guyana, oversaw our trips and made sure we stayed safe and hydrated (he comes by the nickname "Water Nazi" honestly). He helped the trips run smoothly. He deserves much more than thanks.

My husband Don and my two sons John and James were also part of our mission trips. Thankfully, my sons had much better attitudes about the trips than Matt starts out with.

Anil Tejpaul is a Guyanese preacher my congregation helps support. He has always proven to be a gracious host and has a servant's heart.

All the people cited above helped make my trips to Guyana memorable. Those memories played a part in the book. I'll leave it to the reader to guess which incidents cited in Two Weeks in Guyana actually happened in real life.

While I enjoyed writing the book from Matt's point of view, I was concerned about getting his voice right. Connor Patterson, a teenage boy who is an active member of my congregation, read the manuscript and offered helpful suggestions in that area. My thanks to him for his aid.

As with my other books, Tina Seward took on the task of putting on her copyediting hat and going through the manuscript. Any errors that remain are mine alone.

And finally, thanks to my readers who kept asking when my next book was comng out. I hope it was worth the wait.

Two Weeks
in
Guyana

- ONE -

MATT DODGED LOUIS and stepped next to the hoop. His friend Clay tossed the ball to him and he jumped, slamming the dirty basketball into the hoop. "Yes! Score!"

Clay caught the ball before it could bounce out of the pool of light from a fixture on the side of the church building. "Nice one, Matt. Score's three-up, everyone."

Louis grinned good-naturedly. "You're just lucky Robert's not here. This two against one thing isn't fair."

Matt shrugged. "You agreed to play." He glanced out in the gloomy parking lot, where a few people were drifting towards their cars following the Sunday evening services. "Where is he, anyway? I thought I saw him sitting with his family."

Louis caught the ball from Clay and began to dribble it. "He probably went to that meeting they called – you know, for the people who want to go to Guyana this summer?"

"Oh," Matt said, losing interest. He hadn't listened to the announcements at the end of services – he'd been too busy whispering to Clay about a homework assignment. He'd hurried outside after the man leading closing prayer had uttered, "Amen" and when his dad had called his name he'd shouted back he'd be outside shooting hoops.

Matt tried to get the ball away from Louis, who stepped back as he kept control of the ball. "Yeah, Righteous Robert would probably go to a meeting like that," Matt said.

Louis frowned as he tried to get around Clay. "You shouldn't call him that, Matt. It's not very nice. He can't help being the preacher's kid."

Matt rolled his eyes. "Come on, Louis, he always acts like he's so holy and better than us."

Louis opened his mouth to argue and Matt saw his chance. He managed to steal the ball from Louis and, spinning in place, quickly took a shot. It swished in, and Matt laughed.

Louis chased after the ball as it bounced into some bushes that grew next to the church building. Clay wiped his face. "Man, summer . . . that seems like forever from now."

"I know," Matt said. A breeze made him shiver – January in Tampa was pleasant compared to the rest of the country, but that didn't mean it was warm. "But if you talk to my dad, it'll be here before you know it."

"I know it," Clay quipped, and the teenagers shared a laugh. Louis came up with the ball, tossing it to Matt. "My folks are headed for the car. I gotta go."

"See ya," Matt said, trying to spin the basketball on one finger like he saw players do on television. He lost control of it and the ball bounced into the parking lot.

Matt waited for a car to drive by and chased after the old basketball. He grabbed it before it rolled under a parked car.

"Hi, Matt."

He spun around, nervousness making him almost drop the ball again. "Hey, Jenna," he said, wishing he was sweating a little less.

"You weren't at the People Helping People meeting," Jenna said. She was nearly as tall as Matt, with bright blue eyes and curling blond hair caught in a loose ponytail.

"Oh," Matt said, drawing a blank. "I didn't hear about it."

"It was announced tonight," Jenna said. She glanced behind her and Matt saw Mr. and Mrs. Trask heading towards them. "I just figured with your parents at the meeting, you'd be there too."

"Jenna, honey? Let's go," Mrs. Trask called.

Jenna nodded at her parents and turned back to Matt. "Well, I guess I'll see you later," she said.

"Uh, yeah, sure," Matt said. He watched as she walked with her parents to their car.

Smooth, Brooks. Really smooth.

He started to head back to the basketball hoop when he heard his name called. He saw his parents coming across the parking lot, holding hands, which Matt thought was weird at their age.

His dad carried his Bible and a bulging file folder on one arm. "Ready to go, son?" he asked.

"Yeah, just a sec," Matt said. He jogged over to Clay, who was still waiting by the old hoop. "Here ya go," Matt said, shooting the ball to his friend. "Mom and Dad say it's time to go."

Clay grinned as he gave the basketball a hard bounce. "How'd talking to Jenna go? You manage to actually form words?"

"Shut up," Matt said without rancor. "I'll see you in school tomorrow, okay?"

He turned and headed to the family's red Pontiac Grand Am, a car he was just waiting to drive. He'd just turned sixteen and was lobbying for his learner's permit.

He clambered into the backseat as his mother said, "I wish you'd come to the meeting, honey."

The meeting again? "I didn't hear about it," he admitted.

"If you'd paid attention during services, instead of chatting with your friends,you might have known about it," his father said as he got behind the wheel.

"Sorry," Matt said. "Was it a good meeting?"

His parents exchanged a look. "Well, we want to talk to you about it," his father said. "How does Subway sound for dinner?"

"Sounds great!" said Matt. Subway was his favorite restaurant to go to after Sunday evening services.

"Good," his dad said. "We'll talk over dinner."

* * *

After giving thanks for their food, Matt's father began to speak. "Matt, how much have you heard about People Helping People?"

Matt had already taken a huge bite of his meatball sandwich when his father asked his question. He quickly chewed and swallowed. "Um, it's something the church sponsors every year, right? Sending people to some poor country to help out?"

"It's more than that," his mother said. "They send a medical mission team to Guyana, South America each year. The doctors provide medical care and others help out in other ways. Everyone is given an opportunity to obey the gospel."

"Oh. Cool," Matt said. "So, what, they want Dad to go because he's a doctor?"

"Well, that's part of it," his dad said, pushing his glasses up his nose. "Here's the thing, Matt: your mom and I think this would be a great way to spend our vacation this year."

Matt had been about to shovel in a handful of chips when he heard that. He let the chips drop on the wrapping from his sandwich. "You and Dad would go to Guyana for our vacation? What about Disney World?"

"Sweetheart, this is more important than Disney World," his mother said.

Matt slumped back in the booth. "But we live in Florida now," he said. "You said you'd think about us going to Disney World this year since it was only two hours away now instead of two days."

"Disney World will still be there," his dad pointed out. "Besides, you've never been out of the country before – this will be a great experience for you."

"What!" Matt straightened up in his seat, his eyes widening. "Who says I'm going to Guyana?"

"Your mom and I," his father said. "We'd both like to go, and we think you should go as well."

"Wait, don't I get a say in this?" Matt asked. "I don't want to go to some stupid third world country!"

"This will be an excellent opportunity for you," his mother said, putting down her Diet Coke. "You are so blessed, Matt, this will show you how much."

"Just think," his dad said, "it's a chance to share your faith in a foreign country."

Matt looked from one parent to the other. "So that's it? You guys just decide to ruin my summer vacation and I just have to grin and bear it?"

His father's eyes narrowed. "It's only two weeks, son. It won't kill you."

Matt slouched back in his seat, the food in front of him forgotten. "Yeah, right," he muttered.

"Enough," his dad said. "Finish up your dinner and we'll get on home. You'll see, this isn't as bad as you're thinking."

With a sigh, Matt picked up his sandwich and took a bite.His folks thought it was a done deal. He wasn't done arguing. But he'd drop it for now.

But there was no way he was going to waste part of his summer in a lousy third world country. No way.

This wasn't over.

- TWO -

"I CAN'T BELIEVE THEY'RE STILL GONNA DO THIS!" Matt said to Clay as they hung out in his bedroom. Clay was on the floor, fiddling with an Xbox 360 controller while Matt sprawled on his unmade bed, his chin in his hands.

It was June. School had let out the week before, and sunlight streamed in from the window over the oak desk that held Matt's computer.

Clay grimaced. "It sucks, man," he agreed.

From the night in January, when Matt's parents had announced their decision, until now, Matt had been campaigning for them to change their minds. Nothing had worked.

He'd tried arguing. He was fine with his folks going, if that's what they wanted. But why couldn't he stay home alone? He was sixteen years old, it wasn't like he was going to burn the house down.

His parents insisted that he was going.

He'd tried sulking, holing up in his room and tweeting his friends about how lame it all was. He'd given his parents the silent treatment.

They were unmoved and repeated that he was going.

He'd tried to reason with them. He wasn't a missionary or a doctor. He would be useless there.

They promised he'd have stuff to do. He was going.

Now summer vacation had begun and he couldn't enjoy it because he knew that in less than a week he'd be getting on an airplane bound for Guyana. For two stinking weeks.

Now he rolled onto his back and stared at the ceiling. "They just don't care what I want," he told Clay.

"Maybe it won't be so bad," Clay suggested. "It's another country."

"A third world country," Matt said. "And it's gonna be hot and I have to wear a collared shirt the whole time I'm there. We can't even drink the water."

Clay shrugged. "Whatever. You wanna do something besides gripe? Let's play a game or something."

Matt rolled back onto his stomach so he could glare at his friend. "I thought you were on my side."

"Hey, I am. I agree it sucks," Clay said. "But come on, let's try to have a little fun before you have to go. I'm bored."

Matt sighed as he pushed himself off the bed. "Fine," he grumbled. "We'll play something."

Clay gave his friend a sympathetic grin as Matt pulled out Madden NFL 12. "Look at it this way. It's only two weeks."

Yeah, Matt thought. *Gonna be the longest two weeks of my life.*

* * *

Saturday dawned, promising to be a scorcher. Matt grimaced as he pulled on the bright green t-shirt everyone was told to wear that day. On the front was the name of the group, People Helping People. On the back was a drawing of a Bible and the statement, "God Heals – Body and Soul."

Matt took one look at himself in the mirror in his bathroom and wanted to rip the stupid thing off. He felt like a dork, wearing this shirt.

A knock on the door. "You about ready, Matt? We need to get Robert and get on the road," his father said.

"Just a minute," Matt called. Yeah, that was right. They were giving Righteous Robert a ride with them to Miami, where they were going to catch their flight to Guyana. He was going to be in a car with the guy for four hours.

Someone just shoot him, please.

He ran a hand through his reddish-brown hair, wishing it was just a little longer. His mother made him get a haircut the day before and now his ears stuck out. His blue eyes glared at his reflection.

No question about it. He really did look like a dork.

With a sigh he left the bathroom and joined his parents in the den, where their luggage waited to be hauled into his mom's Ford Explorer.

The two weeks couldn't go fast enough.

* * *

"Thanks for picking me up, Mr. and Mrs. Brooks," Robert said as he climbed into the SUV to sit next to Matt.

"No problem, Robert," Matt's mother said. "We're glad you can be part of the trip."

"Yeah, I know my folks wish they could come," Robert answered. "But two weeks is a long time for my dad to be gone from the pulpit and Mom didn't want to leave Cindy after she broke her arm."

"How's your sister doing?" Matt's dad asked.

"Much better, thank you sir," Robert said. He turned to Matt, who had kept his earbuds in his ears while his iPod played music from his favorite German metal group.

Even with that, he could still hear Robert and his folks. Robert talking and acting like the perfect preacher's kid. Now he was looking at Matt with a big grin on his face as he said, "This is gonna be such a great time!"

Matt bit the inside of his cheek to stop the bark of unbelieving laughter that rose in his throat. Instead, he shrugged as he turned up his music.

Robert's smile faltered, then faded away completely. He ran a hand through his blond hair and muttered, "Well, I'm gonna look at the Bible study we're going to use. Have you had a chance to see it, Mrs. Brooks?"

Matt closed his eyes as his mother answered. He concentrated on the swift savage beat that thrummed on his eardrums.

It was going to be a *long* two weeks.

- THREE -

MIAMI INTERNATIONAL AIRPORT WAS HOT, noisy, and crowded. Matt followed along behind his parents, dragging his rolling suitcase behind him.

"There's Stan!" his mother said, pointing. Stan Conner, an elder of the church they attended and the leader of the team, was looking rather harried as he and two college-aged guys were maneuvering a luggage cart piled high with suitcases.

The family and Robert made their way to the group. Matt looked around at the sea of green t-shirts that congregated in this part of the airport. He saw Jenna standing with her parents, all of them decked out in the People Helping People shirts. They looked excited.

"Matt!" His father yanked out one of his earbuds. "Pay attention! Give Stan a hand with those suitcases."

He opened his mouth to protest but the stern look his father gave him made him reconsider. He nodded and followed his dad to where Stan was standing.

The older man was mopping his face with a handkerchief. He managed a grin when he saw Matt and his dad. "David! Matt! Good to see you!"

"Good to be here, Stan," Matt's dad said. He looked over the small mountain of cases. "We have all the medical supplies?"

"Except for the stuff you and Jim were bringing with you," Stan said, glancing at the large black suitcases Matt's dad was pulling. "You going to check that one in yourself?"

"Yeah, if that's not a problem," Matt's dad said.

Matt shook his head as he looked at all the suitcases on the luggage cart. "We need all this stuff?" he asked.

Robert was next to him, and he answered before the adults could. "Yeah, Matt. We've got medicines, books, stuff for the doctors – just wait 'til we get there and you see how we set up a clinic out of nothing!"

Matt grimaced. He didn't want to see it, truth be told. He already wanted to be back in Tampa where he belonged.

Stan turned to one of the college kids. "Chuck, spread the word – we're going to need people to check one of these bags in with their luggage. It's cheaper that way. Find people with only one bag to check in."

Chuck nodded and made his way to the group of people waiting for instructions. Matt noticed the group was getting looks from people passing by. He wished he could crawl into one of the suitcases and hide.

"Okay, guys?" Stan said. "As people are checking in, I want you to get one of these suitcases over to them. Work together, especially on the top ones – I don't want anyone needing a doctor *before* we get to Guyana."

Robert and the other college kid – Matt couldn't think of his name at the moment – laughed at Mr. Conner's joke. Matt just shook his head. He thought about putting his earbuds back on, but he knew if he did, he wouldn't hear any directions. And it seemed his father was already ticked off with him.

For the next half hour Matt helped lug suitcases – and man, the bags were heavy! – to fellow mission workers checking in at the Caribbean Air ticket counter. Everyone seemed excited. They had broad smiles on their face and kept chattering about how great the trip was going to be.

Matt was sick of it. He was here against his will. Everyone else might think this was a great thing. For him it was a prison sentence. And he was already counting the days until it was over.

* * *

Matt found that he had the window seat – 18-F. He settled into it hoping it meant he wouldn't have to talk to anyone for a while.

His dad settled into the seat next to him. "You're not having a very good attitude, son."

"I'm here and I'm quiet," Matt pointed out. "It's not like I wanted to be here."

"Don't you think everyone can see how you feel?" his father was speaking in low tones, hard to hear over passengers around them putting up luggage and finding their seats. "You're going to be down there with us for two weeks – you can keep on how you're acting or you can make the best of it."

"You wanted me to come," Matt said. "I'm doing the best I can."

His father frowned. "I find that hard to believe."

Matt wanted to argue further, but he saw his mother watching him and his dad with anxious eyes. He also realized that, despite the fact they weren't being very loud, others might be aware of the argument.

"Fine," he muttered to his father. "I'll try to do better."

His father looked as if he were going to say something else, but then his wife lay a hand on his arm and whispered something to him Matt couldn't hear. Whatever it was, Matt's dad nodded and turned back to his son. "I hope so. Your mother and I hope you come away from this trip with something more than a bad attitude."

Matt decided it was better to just keep his mouth shut and end the conversation. With a nod to his father, he leaned his head against the window of the plane and closed his eyes.

* * *

Hours later, the plane was landing in Guyana. Matt looked out the window, but it had gotten dark a while ago – all he could see was small lights far below them.

The plane touched down with a light bump, and the flight attendant welcomed them all to Georgetown, Guyana. She spoke with an accent – Matt couldn't quite place it, but it had a Jamaican flavor to it.

The plane taxied for a bit, then finally rolled to a stop. Matt stood and stretched his legs the best he could in the cramped space – he was forced to duck to keep from hitting his head on the panel above him.

"Don't forget your immigration form," his dad told him.

"It's in my pocket," Matt replied. His father had to help him with a number of the answers to the questions the slip of paper asked – where they were staying, for example. The hotel was called the Phoenix, and that would be where they'd sleep for the next two weeks.

Matt grabbed up his backpack and checked for his passport. People were starting to move out of the plane now, and Matt waited with his family for their turn to deplane.

To his surprise, instead of a jetway, there was a flight of stairs pushed up to the plane's door. Matt took a deep breath – *here we go* – and, for the first time, stepped out into a foreign country.

The first thing that hit him was that it wasn't hot. He'd remembered at one meeting that the country wasn't that far from the

Equator – five degrees latitude, Stan had said. He'd figured he'd be sweltering the minute he got off the plane.

Instead, it felt like an early summer evening in Florida – warm, but not uncomfortably so. Matt shrugged as he got to the bottom of the steps. He wondered what other surprises the country had for him.

Everyone was streaming into a one-story building to the right of the plane. Matt followed the group, looking around. There were a couple more planes near his, but no one was coming out of them. The light available didn't let him see much detail beyond that.

The building they entered gave the name of the airport – Cheddi Jagan International Airport. Walking through the open doors, Matt found himself in a large room cooled by several fans placed strategically about. Long lines of people stood waiting to be processed through immigration, which consisted of several booths at the end of the room.

Matt sighed. The lines didn't move quickly. He noticed a man wearing a brown uniform gazing at the line, not a hint of welcome on his dark face as he scanned the people.

Despite the fans, the room was warm. Matt could smell sweat and some sort of smelly hair product from the line next to his. He wrinkled his nose. A woman stood across from him, her hair long braids down her back. She had a baby balanced on one hip and a large black purse in her other hand.

Matt caught himself yawning. He glanced at his watch – 9:15 in the evening. How could he be tired already? He hadn't *done* anything but sit most of the day.

"So?" Robert asked from behind him. "What do you think of your first look at Guyana?"

Matt took in the room, with its hard wooden benches along the walls, the soft jabber of people speaking with that strange accent, the unsmiling guard.

"It's different," he admitted. He didn't really want to talk to Robert but his dad was standing in front of him and probably listening. "I thought it'd be hotter."

"It will be," Robert promised. "Just wait until tomorrow."

Matt nodded, hoping that would be all he'd have to say. Fortunately, Jenna asked Robert a question and he turned to answer her, leaving Matt to his thoughts.

Finally it was his family's turn at one of the booths. The unsmiling woman looked over their paperwork and stamped their passports with a minimum of words. Matt took back his passport and followed his folks to collect their baggage.

"David!" Stan called. "Come here, I want you to meet Steve."

Matt saw that the group leader was talking to a large pale-skinned man near the luggage carrel. The stranger had a salt-and-pepper beard and twinkling brown eyes. He was dressed in slacks and a green checkered shirt.

"David," Stan continued, "This is Steve Lockwood, the missionary we're going to be working with this week. Steve, this is Dr. David Brooks, his wife Emily, and their son Matt."

"Welcome!" Steve said, clasping Matt's father's hand with both his own. "We're grateful to have another doctor join the group. That makes what, five of you now?"

"That's my understanding," Matt's dad said. "I haven't had the chance to really talk yet with Dr. Lopez and Dr. Nelson – I just met them in Miami this morning."

"Don't worry, I'm sure you'll get to know each other quite well before the two weeks are up," Steve said. He turned to Matt and his mom. "And it's always good to have families working together. We'll put you both to good use this week, don't worry."

Matt's mom smiled. "I'm looking forward to teaching the gospel to some of the people here," she said.

Steve grinned. "It's going to be great. The Guyanese are a special people, you'll see why I love them." He clapped Matt on the shoulder. "And it's great to see more young people here! How old are you, Matt?"

"Sixteen," Matt said.

"Youngest of the bunch? Don't worry, you'll have no problem fitting in," Steve said. "Well, I have to go make sure there's no problems with Customs. Don't forget, we'll be meeting in the dining room once you all get to the Phoenix."

Inwardly Matt groaned. It was already nearing 10 PM – when would this day be over?

"Let's grab our luggage," his dad said. "Talk to you later, Stan."

Matt said nothing while they found their bags and went through Customs. He'd found Steve Lockwood a little overwhelming. This man acted like Guyana was a great place to be, a great place to serve God.

Matt didn't see it. He was sure he never would.

- FOUR -

STEVE LOCKWOOD WAS DIRECTING EVERYONE to six dark-blue vans. "Let's get in, folks! I know you're tired, but let's keep moving!"

After dropping his luggage off at the van in the rear, Matt followed his parents to the third van in line. A young man grinned at him as he stood next to the right-hand front door, his teeth bright white under the streetlights.

Matt slid into the middle seat, next to his mother. He looked up front and blinked. The steering wheel and dashboard sat on the right side of the van, not the left like he was used to.

Before he could point this out to his parents his mother spoke up. "No seatbelts," she said, sounding a little worried.

"It's a third world country, Em. I'm sure it'll be fine," his father replied. He was glancing out the window on his side of the van. "I hope they're careful with the bags," he said.

Matt didn't have an answer for either of those statements, so he glanced out his window. Steve Lockwood came to their van and stuck his head in. "Okay, got everyone in your family here, Dave? Don't want to leave someone behind."

"Yes, thank you Steve," Matt's dad said. "They know to be careful with some of the bags, right?"

For the first time Matt saw Lockwood's smile dim. "They know what they're doing, Doctor," he said. "We've done this for the past five years, and I'd like to think we're good at it."

"Of course," Matt's dad said quickly. "I didn't mean to offend you."

Lockwood nodded as he took a headcount of the people in the van. Matt turned around and noticed Jenna and her folks were sitting in the back, along with a couple of adults Matt knew from church.

"Okay, we're about ready to go," Lockwood said, slapping the side of the van. The young man who'd been standing by the door climbed into the driver's seat and turned the ignition key. Matt immediately smelled engine fumes and the van rumbled to life.

Two minutes later, the van in front of them started to move. Matt's van quickly followed. Several turns later they were out of the airport and speeding down a dark road, driving on the left-hand side of the road instead of the right.

At first, Matt found this disconcerting. He was sitting on the right-hand side of the van and it felt wrong to see cars coming up towards them from that side.

It didn't help that the driver was going pretty fast, leaning on his horn now and again sometimes for no reason Matt could see.

Traffic increased as they got into the city. Matt blinked at one point when he saw a cow standing placidly in their lane, forcing them to veer to the right in order to miss it.

His mom gasped next to him. "Did you see that?" she asked.

"Yeah," Matt said. A cow. In the middle of the road in a city. That wasn't something you saw in Tampa.

He glanced back and saw Jenna clutching the edge of her seat, her eyes wide. He wished he could be sitting next to her – maybe even put an arm around her so she wouldn't be so scared.

He snorted to himself. *Get a grip, Brooks. Like that's ever gonna happen.*

Despite the hour, the city seemed busy. People thronged the sidewalks and Matt caught snatches of music and laughter as they passed streets filled with two-story homes and businesses.

Finally, the vans pulled up to a tall building with a sign in front of it: "The Phoenix Hotel." The vans parked and the young man driving quickly jumped out and opened the door for his passengers.

"Thanks," Matt muttered as he climbed out of the van. The wild ride had woken him up some. He wondered if everyone in Guyana drove like a crazy person or just the people in this area.

Matt's dad was talking with Jenna's dad as they walked into the hotel. Matt stole a glance at Jenna. She was speaking with her mom, her face animated now that they were out of the van.

"This way, this way," Stan Conner was saying, waving the group through the large, airy hotel lobby. Matt heard birds chirping as they went through to a high-ceilinged room filled with square tables covered with white linen.

Steve Lockwood was already there, standing at one end of the room. "Come in, have a seat," he said, his smile back in place.

Matt and his folks took seats at a table near the front of the room. Matt didn't like that but slouched down into a seat. Robert took the fourth chair. "So, Mr. and Mrs. Brooks, what do you think so far?"

Matt's dad smiled. "You all didn't exaggerate about the driving here."

"Yeah, isn't it wild?" Robert grinned. "One year a cow apparently died somewhere between the airport and the hotel – man, did it stink!"

Matt's mother shuddered. "It was a little unnerving."

"Hey, no worries, Mrs. Brooks, there's never been an accident with the vans all the times I've been coming on these trips. It's cool."

Before Matt's mom could answer, Steve Lockwood spoke up. "Okay, everyone! If I can have your attention…"

People quieted down and gave their attention to the missionary. He beamed at them. "Okay – welcome! First-timers and repeaters, welcome to Guyana! My job is to help you these next two weeks to make them as profitable as possible."

Matt stuck his hand in his pocket and began to toy with his iPod earbuds. He wished he could slip them on and ignore Lockwood, but that was out of the question with his parents sitting right next to him.

Lockwood began to go over some ground rules for the stay in Guyana. "Now, we'll be collecting your passports and locking them up for you while you're in Guyana. Passports are very valuable here, and we don't want anyone's to be stolen."

Matt felt his mind begin to wander as Lockwood went on. Don't go out by yourself. Don't miss the vans when they come to pick you up. Drink plenty of (bottled) water. Don't do this. Don't do that.

Matt glanced around the room. Others were listening attentively, even Robert, who must have heard all this before. Matt was bored. He wanted this over with so he could go to bed.

Finally, Lockwood wrapped up with a reminder of church services in the morning and instructions to be at the vans ready to go by 8:15 AM. "Stan has your keys and your room assignments. You're all checked in and your luggage will be in your rooms. Good night, everyone! Don't forget to give us your passports!"

"Another line," Matt muttered as they stood. Stan was at a table near the door, room keys (real keys,not the magnetic cards Matt saw all the time at hotels in the United States) in a small pile next to him.

"Hey, it's the last one before shut-eye," Robert said. "Don't know about you, brother, but I'm beat."

"Yeah, I'm pretty tired," Matt admitted. He followed along behind his parents as they waited. When it was their turn, Stan gave them a tired grin. "Okay, David and Emily, your room is . . . " he glanced down at the list, ". . . 417." He handed them each a key.

Matt frowned. "What about me?"

Stan glanced at the list again. "I figured you didn't want to room with your folks Matt. You and Robert will be sharing room 424. Let's have your passport and I'll give you your key."

What? Matt thought. *I don't want to share a room with Righteous Robert!*

Stan glanced at him, his hand out for Matt's passport. He handed it over reluctantly, feeling as if he were giving up a precious bit of freedom along with the document.

"Okay, here you go," Stan said, dropping a key with a maroon tag that had the number "424" stamped on it in gold. "Robert, you heard what I told Matt?"

Matt didn't wait to hear Robert's answer. Ignoring his parents, who were standing by the elevator, he trudged to where the stairs were and climbed up four flights.

When he got to the room, he stared. *This* was one of the nicest hotels in Guyana?

The room was small, taken up mostly by two cots, one on each side of the room. A small desk/vanity sat along the wall to the left, a mirror hanging over it reflecting the beds. Four bottles of water sat on the desk.

There was a television perched on top of a dresser, and a closet next to that. An open ironing board blocked the way to the windows. To the right of that, was a door that Matt assumed led to the bathroom.

Four suitcases were crowded into the room, leaving almost no room to walk. Matt stepped inside, wondering how he and Robert were going to fit in here.

"Hey, man," Robert came up behind him. "Little crowded, huh? It'll be better once we get rid of the medical cases. You want the bed closest to the bathroom or what?"

Matt shot a look at the other teenager. Robert looked tired, but he was still so . . . so enthusiastic about everything. Like this was some great adventure to be experienced instead of something to be endured.

Looking over the room, Matt shrugged. "I don't care. You pick."

"Okay. I'll just bunk here," Robert said, dropping his backpack on the cot to the right. "Let's move some of this stuff so we can get around in here, okay?"

A few minutes later they'd maneuvered the suitcases so that there was a path to the bathroom. Matt took a glimpse inside. It looked like a standard bathroom – white tiled floor, white fixtures, white shower curtain.

"I dunno about you, but I'm just gonna pull out the clothes I'm wearing tomorrow and calling it a night," Robert said.

"Yeah, that sounds good," Matt said. He opened his suitcase and found a pair of dark blue slacks and a red plaid dress shirt. He hung them both in the closet. Robert did the same with his black slacks and ice blue shirt.

A half hour later, with Robert snoring in the bed across from him, Matt lay on his back, thinking. There was Internet here, but his folks had the laptop computer. No Xbox. He hadn't flicked on the television, but he'd bet the shows were terrible.

Just one day in Guyana and he was already homesick.

- FIVE -

MATT WOKE TO THE SOUND of the shower running in the bathroom. He sat up and swung his legs out of bed, rubbing his eyes as he gazed at the small hotel room. It wasn't a bad dream. He was still in Guyana. Great.

The shower stopped. Matt got up and began rummaging in his suitcase for his toothbrush. A few minutes later he heard the bathroom door open behind him.

Robert came out, dressed in the clothes he'd hung up the night before, his blond hair damp. "Afraid there's bad news, Matt. No hot water."

"What?" Matt stared at the other teen. "You're kidding."

"No lie," Robert said. "Makes for a quick shower. I can safely say I'm awake now."

Matt grunted. A cold shower. Great. He grabbed his things and went into the bathroom.

As Robert had said, there was no hot water coming out of the tap. Matt took the fastest shower he'd ever done and came out shivering, grabbing one of the towels and wrapping it around him trying to get warm.

A few minutes later he was dressed and getting ready to brush his teeth. He'd just squirted toothpaste on his toothbrush when there was a knock on the bathroom door. "Come on in!"

Robert came in, two bottles of water in his hands. "You forgot your water," he said, handing Matt one of the bottles.

"Oh. Thanks," Matt said. After putting toothpaste on his toothbrush, he turned the water on in the sink and started to put his brush under the spray when Robert grabbed his wrist.

"Matt, don't! Remember? We have to use bottled water for that. The water isn't safe to ingest."

Matt felt his cheeks grow warm. He did remember, now that Steve had said something. He looked down at his toothbrush and quickly turned off the faucet. "Yeah. Thanks."

Stupid country, he thought as he poured a little bottled water on his toothbrush and brushed his teeth. *Can't even drink the water!*

A few minutes later he was ready to go downstairs for breakfast. Robert had waited for him and they walked downstairs together, Robert chatting about Guyana and Matt trying to ignore him.

Breakfast was in the room they'd met in the night before. Long tables were set up in the front of the room, with a buffet laid out. There were scrambled eggs, bacon, sausage, and toast. A white ceramic bowl held chunks of watermelon.

Matt realized he was starving and piled his plate high. When he got to the end of the buffet line he saw a silver coffeemaker, along with cups. He poured himself a cup of coffee and looked around for some sugar.

"Whatcha need?" Robert asked as he came up behind Matt.

"I don't see any sugar," Matt frowned.

"Oh yeah. Here," Robert picked up a cup that was filled with yellowish-brown crystals. "The sugar here's a little different."

Matt frowned as he spooned some of the odd-looking stuff into his cup. He took a cautious sip. It tasted different, not like his coffee with sugar at home. But it was drinkable, he guessed.

He carried his plate and cup to a table where his mom and dad sat. "Morning, Matt," his mom said as he slid into a chair. "Did you sleep all right?"

"Yeah, Matt said. "But we can't get any hot water in our hotel room. That sucks."

"Yes, we noticed the same thing," his dad said as he sipped his coffee. "I was going to ask someone at the front desk about it."

Matt noticed that Robert had joined a couple of the college-age kids at another table. Robert said something and the two older boys burst out laughing.

Matt wondered if they were talking about him. He quickly dropped his eyes to his plate and began to shovel in scrambled eggs, feeling uneasy.

Stan wiped his mouth on a cloth napkin and stood up. "The vans will be here in a few minutes," he said. "Let's finish up and get ready for worship. Then don't forget this afternoon we'll be making pill packs."

There was a murmur of acknowledgment and Matt took a quick gulp of his coffee. He noticed his parents had their Bibles sitting on the table and remembered he'd left his in his room. He decided that rather than run to his room, he'd used the Bible program on his phone. He could look up things faster with it anyway.

A few minutes later everyone was climbing into the dark blue vans again. Matt took a quick moment to look up and down the street. He noticed what appeared to be a grocery store across the street with a Chinese restaurant next to it. People were strolling down the dusty street and Matt could tell it was going to be a hot day.

He climbed into a van and found himself next to Robert. The other teen was looking a little sheepish. "Hey, Matt – I owe you an apology, man."

Matt flushed a little. He recalled Robert sitting with the college kids and their laughter. "Yeah?"

"Yeah," Robert nodded. "I forgot – the hot water was working. You have to turn on both faucets to full to get it running." He jerked his chin to where the two college boys were laughing and getting into the van in front of them. "Brad and Chuck reminded me about it at breakfast. Boy, do I feel like an idiot."

Matt thought about a number of responses he could make. He settled for, "Okay. Anything else I need to know you forgot to tell me?"

Robert shrugged. "Dunno. We'll see." He looked over at Jenna and her family as they took seats in front of them. "Hey, Jenna. Hey, Mr. and Mrs. Trask."

Matt slipped his earbuds on and turned on his iPod. He'd just tune out the drive this time until they got to church.

Once they got going though, Matt found it impossible not to gawk. Traffic at one point was literally bumper-to-bumper, and Matt stared as he saw a man calmly climb over the nearly touching bumpers of the vans in order to cross the street.

The city was teeming with life. The vans shared the road with bicycles and at least two horse drawn carriages. They passed a house with a yard full of squawking chickens that was next to a storefront of some kind.

Billboards advertised brands Matt had never heard of. He saw one for Kentucky Fried Chicken and wondered where the restaurant was. Some things apparently crossed borders.

They slowed down as they approached a bridge. Matt craned his neck to get a better look at it. Robert said something that he didn't catch, so he flipped off one of his earbuds. "What?"

"It's a pontoon bridge," Robert said. "US Army Corps of Engineers built it."

"It floats," Jenna added from the seat in front of them. "It's a neat bridge, but a little scary."

"Scary?" Matt asked.

"You'll see," Robert said with a grin.

They'd gone a little ways on the bridge when Matt saw the sign. It was white with black letters and it warned:

MAINTAIN SPEED

LOOSE BOARDS

BRIDGE UNDER REPAIR

Matt blinked. "Loose boards?"

"We don't know what it means," Robert said. "Never been an accident here though. Not with the vans. Jenna just thinks the sign makes it scary."

"It does!" Jenna said, blushing slightly.

Matt felt the bridge rattle under the van. He thought about loose boards and wondered how worried he should be. But the driver hid his concern well so Matt decided not to freak out about it.

He wondered how different the church service would be. And if he'd ever quit feeling homesick.

- SIX -

THE AREA THEY WERE DRIVING IN now was a lot more rural than Georgetown. Matt saw fields of sugarcane flash by. Muddy water ran through ditches on either side of the road.

Finally the vans pulled up to a small one-story building the color of sand. A fence surrounded it, and a small sign nailed to the fence read "Demarara Church", with times of services listed below. Next to the building was what looked like an unfinished carport, with beams holding up a partial roof. A set of wooden planks had been laid over the ditch, providing access to the building.

Matt watched as Jenna clutched her father's arm as she went over the planks. He crossed after them, noting that a couple appeared to be loose.

Small children ran around the front of the building, dressed in brightly colored clothes. Two young boys stopped and looked at Matt and Robert, huge grins on their faces.

"Hey, guys," Robert said. The boys giggled and ran off. Matt fought his own grin as he continued inside the dim building.

Two rows of hard wooden benches sat on either side of the large room. In front there were two tables, each covered with a white tablecloth. One was piled with old songbooks and Bibles, while the other held a silver communion set.

Stan embraced one of the men who stood near the front. He had black hair and a complexion that reminded Matt of pictures he'd seen of Indians in India.

The man held a Bible and wore a tie with his tan dress shirt and dark slacks, and Matt wondered if he were the preacher. Stan was talking to the man and gesturing to the People Helping People members as he did.

"Who's Stan talking to?" Matt's dad asked Robert as they moved to a bench near the back of the room.

"That's Brother Harry, the preacher here at the Demarara Church," Robert answered. He slipped into the bench in front of the Brooks family and turned towards him as they sat. "We support his family from Tampa."

Matt watched as people took their seats around him. He saw one of the small boys from outside grin at him, white teeth flashing against his dark skin. Laughing, the child scampered to a pew in front where he climbed on a heavy lady's lap.

Stan took a seat in front as Harry spoke up. "It's time to begin our worship service. We are pleased to have Brother Stan and the members of People Helping People here with us today. We are grateful for the good work they do and look forward to helping them out these next two weeks. Let us pray."

Matt obediently bowed his head but kept his eyes open. Harry's accent made it hard to understand everything he was saying, but he managed to get the gist of the prayer. It was for a lot of people to be seen and a lot of souls to be saved over the next two weeks.

After the congregation said "Amen," Harry picked up one of the songbooks that sat on the table. "Let's turn to number 223 – "Amazing Grace."

At Harry's direction, the people began to sing the words of the well-known hymn. Matt saw his mom's eyes fill as she sang in her clear alto. He shifted in his seat, as a feeling he couldn't describe welled in him.

This was a different country, a different people. The people's accents gave the words a foreign flavor. But it was still "Amazing Grace," a song Matt had sung countless times back in the States.

He didn't understand the feeling until some of the young men began to pass out the Lord's Supper. As he broke off a piece of cracker, it dawned on him that not just here, but in Tampa they would be doing this today. And not just in Tampa, but places like this all over the world – brothers and sisters in Christ, sharing this memorial meal together.

He was starting to feel a kinship with these Guyanese men and women.

Matt swallowed the small cup of grape juice and tried to push the thought aside. It didn't matter. Yeah, it was a cool insight but it didn't mean that he *wanted* to be here. Home still looked pretty good from his perspective.

Matt listened to the sermon, using the Bible program on his Droid phone to look up verses. He saw some of the kids staring at him and wondered if they thought he was playing a game. That bothered him, even though he tried not to let it.

Finally the service came to an end. Matt felt some relief. Despite the fact that all the doors had been opened in the crowded building for ventilation, the temperature was steadily rising.

Matt's mom used an old church bulletin she'd found in her Bible to fan herself. "That was so moving!" She followed Matt out of the bench.

Matt didn't say anything, just let his mom talk to his dad while he tried to make his way outside. Several of the Guyanese said hello to him and shook his hand, and Matt was forced to introduce himself over and over again before he escaped out the double doors.

Jenna was outside. She was wearing a white blouse and a floral print skirt and laughing as she talked to some of the children. She shot Matt a shy smile. "What did you think of services?"

Matt shrugged. "It was a church service," he said.

He saw her face fall slightly and wished he'd said something different. But talking about his feelings from the service just felt . . . dorky to him. He didn't want to be like that in front of Jenna.

One of the girls, her black hair done in small braids, pointed at Matt. "That boy be playing games during church. I saw him."

"No," Matt said, his face getting red as Jenna looked surprised. "It's a Bible program. Look." He pulled out his phone and showed Jenna.

"You brought your phone?" she asked.

"Yeah," Matt said. "Habit, I guess. No service here, obviously."

Jenna nodded as she pulled out a pink phone from her small hand purse. "I know what you mean. Plus I have games on my phone. And a camera."

"Camera? Take my picture!" the girl with the braids said, grinning widely.

Jenna smiled and did as she was asked. She showed the picture to the child, who started giggling. Other children demanded that their pictures be taken as well, and Jenna was soon busy snapping photos and showing them to the children, who laughed as if it were the funniest thing they'd ever seen.

Matt watched the scene, feeling a little envious. Jenna was obviously happy to be here. She appeared to be having as much fun as the kids were.

Part of him wished he could feel that way too.

- SEVEN -

EVERYONE IN THE VAN on the way back was animated, talking about the services and how much they were looking forward to the next two weeks. Everyone, that is, except Matt.

He found himself oddly depressed, the feeling he'd had during services gone as if he'd never experienced it. It seemed everything around him reminded him that he wasn't home, where he really wanted to be.

Part of it was seeing how easy Jenna was with it. Part of it was the temperature, which was steadily climbing during the half hour drive back to the hotel – and, of course, the van didn't have air conditioning.

Matt watched as a half dozen goats strolled by the van as they waited to make a left turn. It all felt so strange to him. Cars drove on the wrong side of the road. Animals roamed freely without anyone batting an eye. They drove by a brewery, and Matt's nose wrinkled at the sharp scent of brewing beer.

He wished he were home. He didn't like this feeling of being an outsider, apart from everyone and everything. He belonged in Tampa. Why hadn't his folks just left him there?

Once back at the hotel, Matt and Robert hurried to their room to wash up before lunch. Robert was cheerful, talking about how great it had been to see some of the Guyanese people again. "I talk to Harry with Skype sometimes," Robert said as he scrubbed his hands. "It's not the greatest connection sometimes, but we have good discussions."

Matt scratched at a mosquito bite on his arm but said nothing. He quickly washed his own hands and followed Robert down to the dining room.

Lunch was baked chicken, rice, and cooked vegetables. Someone had placed several two-liter bottles of Coca Cola at the end of the table, and Matt poured himself a glass, finding that the sight of the familiar soda made him feel even more homesick.

"Are you drinking enough water?" his mother asked him as he sat at their table. "You know what Steve said about drinking enough water . . . "

Matt fought not to roll his eyes. "Yes, Mom. I'm drinking plenty." He pulled a water bottle from the side of the waistpack he wore and showed her it was half full.

Matt's dad nodded as he swallowed a bite of chicken. "Just make sure you drink up. Dehydration isn't something to fool around with here."

"I know, Dad," Matt said. He shoved the bottle back in its holder and took a grateful sip of Coke.

After lunch was cleared, Steve Lockwood came into the room. He smiled at everyone. "I hope you all have had a good day so far? Great, because it's time to get to work. If some of the young men will help us get the medications in, we'll get started."

Matt got up, along with Robert and the college guys, and they spent the next few minutes hauling in suitcases and boxes. When he was finished he noticed his parents had moved to sit with one of the other doctors and his wife. Matt sat back at the table he'd eaten lunch at and was quickly joined by Robert, Chuck, and Brad. "Mind if we sit here?" Robert asked.

Matt did mind, but he clamped his mouth shut and shrugged. Steve and the drivers of the vans opened up the boxes and suitcases and began placing large bottles of pills on the tables, along with plastic trays, small plastic bags, and spatulas.

"Okay," Steve said. "We need to break these down into pill packs. You need to count out a month's worth of pills – for most of these that'll be 30 – and place them into a baggie. Write on the label what you've put into the bag. When you're done with a bottle, bring it to me and we'll give you another one. Any questions? Okay, let's get started."

Matt looked at the large white bottle in front of him. The label read "pre-natal vitamins." He opened it up and tipped out large brown pills onto the plastic tray.

It was simple enough: count out thirty, slide them into a plastic bag, write on the label. Repeat. Matt wondered if the next two weeks would be this mindless.

Robert, Chuck and Brad laughed and talked as they filled their baggies. They tried to draw Matt into the conversation. But they were talking about last year's trip to Guyana and college life in Tennessee and Matt couldn't work up any interest in either subject. He pulled out his earbuds and flicked on his iPod, tuning everyone out and going through the motions of making pill packs.

* * *

Later that evening, everyone met on the roof of the hotel.

Someone had set up a bunch of folding chairs on the roof. To get there, you had to take an elevator to the top floor, then climb a flight of stairs. Matt skipped the elevator and walked all the way up.

Stars sprinkled the clear sky above. Matt took a swallow of water and thought of a Scripture in the book of Psalms: "The heavens declare the glory of God; and the firmament sheweth His handiwork."

He looked across the roof and saw the lights of Georgetown. A warm breeze blew, bringing the smells of engine exhaust and cooking meat. Though it was close to nine o'clock at night, the city showed no sign of shutting down.

Others drifted into the area. Some of the older folk took seats right away, while a few walked to the edge of the roof and looked out as Matt did. Jenna was one of those. She placed her hands on the parapet and looked across the city. "It's so pretty," she said softly.

Matt felt tongue-tied. He wanted to say something clever and witty back, but settled for a brief "Yeah" as he gulped down more water.

Robert came to stand next to them. "All those people . . . and so many of them need to hear the gospel message," he said.

"It makes me feel so small," Jenna replied. "Like, can we really make a difference in these two weeks?"

Robert rested his arms on the brick parapet. "Even if we only change one life, we'll make a difference. Each soul is a victory."

Matt struggled not to snort. Robert was getting all "churchy" now, and Matt found it irritating. He left the edge of the roof and found a seat near the back, and he tilted his chair back as he fished for his iPod.

Before he could slip his earbuds on, Stan was calling for everyone to take a seat so they could get the devotional started. Chuck and Brad came to sit near Matt, but ignored him as they continued their conversation.

As soon as everyone was seated, Stan led the group in the song, "The Steadfast Love of the Lord." Matt sang with everyone else, but he was on autopilot. His mind was far from the words of the song, too busy feeling sorry for himself.

After two more songs, Stan talked for a few minutes about the reason they were in Guyana. "Jesus said, in Matthew 28:19-20, 'Go ye therefore, and teach all nations, baptizing them in the name of the Father, and of the Son, and of the Holy Ghost: Teaching them to observe all things whatsoever I have commanded you: and, lo, I am with you always, even unto the end of the world. Amen.' While we'll be meeting physical needs this week, don't forget our main purpose – to share the Good News with everyone we can."

"Amen," some people called out.

Matt fiddled with his water bottle. It sounded so noble, the whole, "preaching the gospel" thing. Truth was, Matt didn't have a lot of experience sharing his faith with people. While he knew a number of Bible verses, he just wasn't comfortable talking about that kind of stuff with his non-Christian friends, let alone total strangers.

After Stan spoke a few more minutes, Matt's dad led everyone in a prayer, and the group broke up for the evening. Matt sat for a while, watching everyone else smiling and talking about how great tomorrow was going to be as they started their mission work in earnest.

All Matt could think about was that the sooner they started, the sooner they'd finish, and he could finally go home.

He couldn't wait.

- EIGHT -

ONDAY DAWNED WITH A PROMISE of heat, the humidity
putting Florida to shame. Matt grimaced as he climbed
into one of the vans. This was not going to be a pleasant day.

By the time the vans got to the church building – about 10:30
in the morning – Matt was already sweating. He noticed that even
though the clinic was not officially opening until noon, there was
already a line of people waiting for them.

Harry was already there, a broad smile on his face. "Glad
you're here!" he said over and over again as people got out of the
vans. "Some of us started to move the benches already, we could use
some help."

Stan nodded and gestured to Matt and Robert. "You two give
Harry a hand while the rest of us start unloading the vans."

For over an hour Matt was kept busy. After he and Robert
helped stack benches against the walls, they worked under Stan's
direction setting up partitions in the large room. By the time they
were finished, they'd set up five exam rooms, one for each doctor.
There was also a place for the nurses to get vital signs before the
patients saw a doctor.

Some chairs and benches were set up in the carport-like area for people to sit and conduct Bible studies. Matt, Robert and Stan managed to pull a blue tarp over the unfinished part of the roof to protect those outside. A table and bench were placed in front of the gate where patients would first check in.

"Hey, Matt," Stan said. They were standing in a small partitioned area that was designated the "break room." Here there were two large dispensers – one filled with distilled water, the other with Gatorade. There were also a few chairs where people could sit and quickly gulp down lunch – canned or packaged stuff brought from the States.

"Yeah?" Matt asked as he refilled his water bottle.

"I was wondering if you'd mind helping Jenna, Susie, and Nancy out with the kids today?" Stan asked. "Unless you were planning on being part of the Bible studies."

"No, I wasn't," Matt said. He felt his heart thump down to his shoes. Babysitting? That's what he was going to do for the next two weeks? Really?

"Great," Stan said. "I appreciate your willingness to help." He clapped Matt on the shoulder and then left the break room.

Matt was glad Stan hadn't expected a reply to that. Truth was, he wasn't willing – he was only here because his parents had forced the issue. And the last thing he wanted to do was watch a bunch of whiny kids while their parents saw the docs.

But once again, he had no choice. That seemed to be the mantra of the week. He was stuck in a third-world country, sweating like crazy and forced to slave under a broiling sun. Babysitting, no less.

Two weeks. It was going to feel like two long years.

He left the break room.

* * *

". . . thank you for each person here, and for the great love you showed us by sending your Son to die on the cross for our sins. In His name we pray. Amen," said Robert.

"Amen," everyone echoed. They were standing together in a tight circle, holding hands. Matt quickly dropped his mother's and Mrs. Trask's hands and wiped the sweat off his forehead. His plaid shirt was sticking to his back. Why couldn't they at least wear shorts while working here?

He saw his dad, dressed in green scrubs, head for one of the exam rooms. His mother went over to her husband and gave him a quick kiss on the cheek before she went outside to where the Bible studies would be conducted. Robert followed behind her, flipping open his Bible as he walked.

With a sigh, Matt followed Jenna and the two college girls outside behind the check-in table. They would attempt to entertain the children here. Matt glared up at the bright sun, which seemed to glare right back at him. Some clouds scudded across the pale blue sky – Matt hoped they would block out the golden orb at some point and give him some relief.

It wasn't long before he and the girls were surrounded by a group of bouncy kids. None of them appeared sick to Matt – they seemed to have incredible amounts of energy.

Jenna handed Matt a small bottle of bubble solution. "Here," she said. "Let's blow bubbles for them for a while."

Matt felt stupid at first blowing soap bubbles. But the kids quickly responded to the brightly colored bubbles, laughing and chasing them as they floated in the muggy air. Their laughter was contagious, and Matt found himself grinning as they played.

"Okay," Jenna said after a bit. "Who knows how to play, 'Duck, Duck, Goose?'"

Several of the kids raised their hands and shouted. Matt watched as Jenna and the girls swiftly organized the children into a loose circle for the children's game. Jenna smiled at Matt. "Why don't you play with the kids, Matt?"

He blinked. "Seriously?"

"Yeah!" several of the children cheered.

Jenna nodded. "They like it when an older kid plays."

Matt shifted from foot to foot. "You gonna play?"

She gestured to the light blue skirt she wore. "Hard to play and stay decent."

He wanted to say no. The last thing he wanted to do was play a stupid kid's game.

"Come on, Matt, don't be a party pooper," Nancy said. She flipped back her black braid. "Go ahead and play."

Rolling his eyes, Matt stomped to the circle and flung himself down on the grass. The kids giggled. Matt looked at them, mostly dressed in t-shirts and shorts, and envied their attire.

Children came and went over the next hour. Matt quickly got sick of "Duck, Duck, Goose." The kids loved to pick him to chase them around the circle, and even though he deliberately ran slow so the kid didn't get caught, the efforts caused him to sweat even more.

Clouds finally covered the sun, to Matt's relief. That relief quickly turned to chagrin when a rainstorm erupted and they were suddenly drenched. Jenna and the girls quickly began herding the kids to where the Bible studies were being held, Matt trudging along after them.

He saw his mom talking with a brown-skinned Guyanese woman who was bouncing a baby on her knee while she nodded at something his mom said. Robert stood up and shook the hand of an elderly man who walked slowly to him, clutching a paper in his hand.

Matt stood near the edge of the room, watching Jenna and the other girls corralling the kids. He knew he should lend a hand, but it was crowded under the tarp and he thought he'd just be in the way.

A stiff breeze blew through the area. Matt shivered, his wet clothes making him chilled. Another gust of wind, and the tarp above him rippled.

Matt glanced up as a corner of the tarp gave way. Water had pooled on that part of the tarp, and it was all dumped on Matt. He sputtered, now totally drenched.

The children shouted with laughter at the sight. He noticed Susie and Nancy were laughing as well, and Jenna was trying to hide her smile. Some of those conducting Bible studies also saw what happened and were grinning.

"Hey, Matt, that's one way to stay cool," Brad called out. That caused others to laugh harder.

Matt scowled. Everyone thought it was a big joke, but he was miserable. Without a word he marched off to the break room, hoping no one else was there. He wanted to be left alone.

* * *

After they'd closed down the clinic for the day, they'd dragged back some of the benches to the middle of the room. Lights were strung up and plugged in.

"This is a lot better than last year," Robert told Matt as they finished setting up the room. "They just got electricity here this past year. Last time we were here we had to use a generator."

Matt said nothing. He couldn't care less about what had happened there last year.

"Hey, you all right?" Robert asked.

"Great," Matt grunted. He really didn't want to talk to Robert. He didn't want to talk to anyone.

An hour after the clinic had shut down, people returned for the scheduled religious service. After a time of singing religious songs and prayer, Stan led the gospel meeting, talking about how Jesus went about healing the sick but also teaching them the good news.

"That's what we hope to do these next two weeks," he said. "Not only heal the physically sick, but the spiritually ill as well."

Matt only half-listened to the message. His stomach rumbled. Lunch had been a can of cold pasta with tomato sauce – there was no way to heat up the food at the clinic site.

Once the meeting was over, Matt got up and wandered outside. He knew he should help out with moving things back, but he desperately wanted some alone time. Just get away from everyone.

He walked a little ways down the road. Under the moonlight he could see a large building down the road. His footsteps kicked up dust in the road as he passed the vans. The drivers were nowhere to be seen. Fine with him.

Matt brooded as he walked. He was hot, he was sticky, his arms were covered in bug bites. The restrooms here were primitive – you had to pour water into the toilet to get it to flush.

What had his parents been thinking, dragging him to this sad excuse for a country? It would be good for him? So far all it had been was terrible. He hated it.

And there were almost two weeks left to go.

Matt glanced up and realized he'd walked quite a ways. It was very quiet. Turning, he hurried back towards the church building.

His heart sank as it came into view. The vans were all gone. Only a small car remained, and it was starting to pull out.

"Hey! Wait!" he shouted, running. The car pulled to a halt, and Harry got out of the car. He looked shocked to see Matt hurrying towards him.

Matt looked around, frantic. "Where is everyone?"

"They all went back," Harry said. "They've gone back to the hotel. Why aren't you with them?"

"I – I took a walk," Matt stammered, panic beginning to build.

He'd been left behind. In a third world country, he'd been left behind in the middle of nowhere.

He hadn't wanted to be alone *this* badly.

- NINE -

Harry opened the back door to his car. Matt saw two kids, a boy and a girl, peek out at him.

"Come on," Harry said, "I'll drive you back to the hotel."

Matt hesitated. He was uncomfortable going anywhere with the Guyanese man. He appeared okay – he was a preacher after all – but still, he was a relative stranger.

Then he recalled the orientation Steve Lockwood had conducted Saturday evening. He'd mentioned what to do if you got left behind. One thing not to do was to accept a ride from one of the Guyanese. Matt didn't remember why, but Lockwood had stressed it pretty heavily.

"Um," Matt realized Harry was still waiting for him to get in the car. "That's okay. But, uh, I have to get in touch with Steve Lockwood, I guess."

"Ah, okay," Harry said. He pulled out a battered-looking cell phone from his pocket. "I have his number. I can call him if you want."

"Yeah," Matt said. His own phone wouldn't make calls in Guyana. And given what he was sure Lockwood's reaction would be, he'd much rather Harry talked to him.

It didn't take long before Harry was speaking rapidly into his phone. Due to Harry's accent, Matt had trouble following his end of the conversation. He shifted from foot to foot, feeling the darkness press in on him.

Harry hung up his phone. "Steve is on his way. We'll wait with you."

"Oh, no, sir, you don't have to do that," Matt stammered. Embarrassment was creeping in and the last thing he wanted to do was put anyone else out.

"No, no, it's no problem," Harry said. He reached into the car to turn it off. "This is my wife, Carmen, and my children, Thomas and Ruth. What is your name?"

Matt introduced himself. Harry nodded, repeating his name. Carmen gave him a reassuring smile. The kids grinned, the boy adding a small wave.

A small silence settled between them. Matt heard insects humming and the distant lowing of a cow. No traffic sounds. No sign of anyone coming by anytime soon.

"Uh . . . how old are your kids?" Matt asked. He didn't feel comfortable standing there in the dark silently.

"Ten and twelve," Harry replied. "How old are you?"

Matt scratched at one of a number of bites on his arm. "Sixteen."

"This is your first time here in Guyana?"

"Yeah," Matt nodded.

Harry leaned against the car, appearing comfortable. "It is very different from America, yes?"

Matt nodded, praying Harry wouldn't ask what he thought of Guyana. He was afraid he'd tick the man off enough that he'd leave Matt alone there. And while Matt didn't think of himself as a coward, the thought of being alone there made his mouth go dry.

If Harry noticed his discomfort, he chose to ignore it. "I hear many stories about America. Someday I'd like to go there, if the Lord allows. It sounds like a fascinating country."

"I miss it," Matt let slip out. He bit his lip, not wanting to reveal anything else.

"I can understand that," Harry said. "I know I miss my home when I am away."

Matt didn't know what to say to that, so he leaned against the car next to Harry. He wiped his sweaty face and wished Lockwood would hurry up and get there. Then he thought about the probable reception he'd get from Lockwood and was less eager for the man to get there.

Time crawled by. Harry talked about how the day had gone. "We are grateful for your help here. Already we had three baptisms today."

"We did?" Matt hadn't known. He'd been kept busy with the kids the whole long afternoon.

"Yes," Harry said. "God is working here through you and the others."

Matt fell silent again. He didn't see God working through him – more like God working against him. Otherwise, why was he standing here in the dark in a strange country when he could be at home?

Finally headlights became visible down the road. A white Land Rover pulled up and Steve Lockwood stuck his head out the window. "Good evening, Harry. Thank you for waiting with him."

Harry shrugged. "Good evening, Brother Steve. It was no problem. I offered to drive him to the hotel but he said to call you."

Lockwood's gaze flicked to Matt and his mouth tightened. He looked back at Harry. "He was following instructions. I'll let you and your family get on home now. Thanks again."

Harry shook Steve's hand, then stuck his hand out to Matt. "I'll see you tomorrow, Matt. Have a good night."

Matt shook the preacher's hand and then reluctantly climbed into the left-hand seat. He fastened his seat belt and prepared for the drive back.

Steve said nothing to Matt until Harry drove off. He then performed a Y turn and started back towards Georgetown. "Why did you miss the vans?"

Matt had his arms folded across his chest. He couldn't meet Lockwood's eyes. "I went for a walk."

"You were told to stay on site. You didn't."

"I wanted to take a walk. I didn't think it was a big deal."

"Not a big deal?" Steve repeated. "You've inconvenienced a number of people because of your selfishness. Harry and his family, myself – not to mention worrying your parents. That sounds like a big deal to me."

Matt frowned. He stared out the window, watching the fields and houses flash by.

"I've been watching you," Lockwood continued, "You've come here with a chip on your shoulder. What is your problem?"

Matt grit his teeth. "My parents made me come."

"Oh, poor baby," Lockwood said, his voice dripping sarcasm. "So you've decided to take it out on everyone? Why not make the best of it? You're here, you can choose what kind of attitude to have."

Matt swallowed back hot words. He continued to stare out the window.

"What kind of example do you think you're setting?" Lockwood continued. "You're representing Christ here. Is this the way Jesus would act?"

Matt refused to answer. What did Lockwood know about it? He apparently *liked* being in Guyana. No one had made the missionary come here; he'd chosen it. Matt hadn't been given a choice.

Lockwood kept up the lecture the entire way back to the Phoenix. Matt tried to tune him out. He got the gist of it: Matt was a terrible, selfish person who should just smile and accept that he was stuck here.

It's not fair, Matt thought.

They finally got to the hotel. Before Matt could get out of the car, Lockwood put a hand on his shoulder. "You need to think about what I'm saying, Matt. What you're doing here matters. You can glorify God, or bring reproach on His name. It's up to you."

Matt said nothing, pulling away from the older man. He was starving. He hoped there was still something to eat in the dining room.

His father was waiting for him in the doorway of the dining room. "Matt!" What happened?"

"I just took a walk," Matt said as he tried to go by.

His father grabbed his arm. "Matt, listen to me. Your bad attitude is obvious to everyone here. You know better than this. You need to change your outlook."

That did it.

Matt had already suffered a lecture from Lockwood for the past half hour. His dad starting in on him was the straw that broke the camel's back.

He pulled away from his father. "Look, I didn't want to come here! You and Mom made me! I hate this stinking country, and I hate you!"

Bile in his throat, Matt turned on his heel and stomped off to his room, his anger overpowering his appetite.

- TEN -

MATT SLAMMED THE DOOR to his room and flung himself on his cot. His stomach was in knots and he found it hard to breathe.

The confrontation with his father left Matt shaking. He could count on the fingers of one hand the number of times he'd shouted at his parents. But he'd never done so in public. Never with an audience.

Matt wrapped his arms around himself and stared at the cream-colored wall. He'd recalled how the mutter of voices in the dining room had died off after he'd shouted. His father had called his name when Matt turned and left, but didn't come after him. Part of Matt wished he had.

As his anger died down, Matt felt guilt eating at him. He really didn't hate his father. Yes, he was mad at him for dragging Matt to Guyana. That hadn't changed. But that didn't mean he hated him.

Did he hate Guyana? He lay there staring at the wall, running the question through his mind. It felt like he hated the place. But was he being fair?

His head started to throb. Matt rolled onto his back. The room, crowded with his and Robert's things, seemed impossibly small. It was warm – he hadn't bothered to turn on the air-conditioning when he'd come in.

He got out of bed and turned the wall unit on. He then went into the bathroom and looked at himself in the mirror. His face was red and to his horror he saw tears sparkling in his eyes.

Matt washed his face, relishing the cool water on his burning face. He glanced at his watch. The nightly devo was going to start soon, but he didn't think he'd be welcome after his outburst. He wondered if Robert would show up beforehand. Matt hoped not. He wasn't up to talking to anyone, much less Righteous Robert.

Matt picked up the remote and flipped through the television channels. Many of them were just snow. One was a popular U.S. TV sitcom Matt never watched. The rest looked like local programming or news, and Matt just wasn't interested. He turned the television off and dropped the remote on the cluttered nightstand.

He threw his arm over his eyes and tried to stop thinking for a while.

* * *

Matt opened his eyes and realized he must have dozed off. A glance at his watch said it was close to 10 PM. His stomach rumbled, reminding him that he skipped dinner.

He swung his legs off the cot and wondered if there would be anything to snack on downstairs. There was, of course, his stash of canned food in his suitcase, but he wanted to get out of the room for a bit – it felt like it was closing in on him.

Making sure he had his room key in his pocket, Matt stepped out into the hallway. Everything was quiet and it was deserted. Matt headed for the stairs.

He'd started downstairs when he heard voices above him. The stairwell distorted them but he recognized Robert's voice. And Jenna's.

" – don't know what I should do," Robert was saying. "I mean, do I try to talk to him? Ignore him?"

"I don't get it," Jenna was saying. "Why is he acting like this?"

Matt froze. The voices paused on the landing above him. Matt could hear every word clearly.

"I mean, I get that he didn't want to come and all, but why try to make it miserable for everyone else?" Robert continued. "And to say he hated Guyana in front of everyone? Did you see the looks on their faces?"

"I thought he was a lot nicer than that, but he's being such a jerk," Jenna answered. "I don't know if I ever want to speak to him again."

Matt felt as if he'd been slapped. Had he been acting that badly?

"We can pray for him," Robert said. "I think that's all we can do at this point."

"Maybe you can room with someone else," Jenna said.

"No, I won't do that. But I think I'll give him space tonight. Thanks for listening to me, Jenna."

Matt quietly went back into the hallway, his appetite gone again. He slunk to his room and lay down on his cot, facing away from the door. When Robert came in a few minutes later, Matt shut his eyes and pretended to be asleep.

Later, when Robert's snores alerted him to the fact that his roommate was asleep, Matt found himself tossing and turning. He couldn't get Jenna's words out of his mind.

He's being such a jerk. I don't know if I ever want to speak to him again.

He liked Jenna. He cared about what she thought. The fact she felt that way about him . . .

Matt realized his outburst might have cost him a lot more than he thought. The question was, could he fix things?

* * *

When Matt woke up the next morning, Robert was already dressed and ready to go downstairs. He wished Matt a good morning then hurried out of the room.

Matt took his time. He knew he would have to face everyone after what he'd said last night but he found himself reluctant to do so. What was everyone thinking? Were they all agreeing with Jenna?

Hunger drove him downstairs and into the dining room. The first people he saw when he entered were his parents. They both looked somber as they picked at their food.

Swallowing, Matt knew he had to make things right with them. He walked up to the table and asked, "Dad? Can I talk to you?"

His father looked up and nodded. "Of course, son." He got up and followed Matt to short hallway outside the dining room.

Matt felt his face burning. He looked down at his feet as he said, "I'm sorry I yelled at you last night. It was wrong of me. I don't really hate you."

His father reached out and pulled Matt into a quick hug. "I know you don't. I forgive you, but there are going to be some consequences to your outburst. You realize that."

Matt looked up, surprised. "Consequences?" He'd thought his apology would be enough.

"Not from us," his father said. "Steve Lockwood wants to speak with us before we leave."

"Oh," Matt swallowed. He remembered the stern missionary from last night and wondered what the man had in store to make Matt's life more miserable than it already was.

His stomach rumbled, and his father's lips twitched. "Let's get some food into you before he gets here. Sounds like you could use some."

Matt agreed and followed his father into the dining room. He noticed that, aside from his mother, everyone on the mission team was avoiding looking at him. The Guyanese in the room, on the other hand, glanced at him long enough to frown or glare before pointing their gazes elsewhere, their chins raised.

Matt couldn't decide which reaction bothered him more.

He choked down his bacon and scrambled eggs while sitting with his folks. They didn't push him to talk, something he was grateful for. He just listened as his dad spoke about some of the patients he'd treated the day before.

Matt had just finished off his toast when Steve Lockwood came into the dining room. The missionary's eyes narrowed when he saw Matt. He gestured to him and his parents, indicating he wanted to talk with them.

His feet feeling like lead, Matt followed Lockwood out of the dining room, his parents behind him, wondering what kind of consequences Steve Lockwood might have in mind.

- ELEVEN -

D O YOU HAVE ANY IDEA how offensive you were last night?"
Matt winced at Lockwood's tone but continued to
stare at his shoes. He was sitting on his mom's bed – his parents had
offered their room as place for this meeting, something Matt was
grateful for. At least he wasn't being reamed out in public.

"Matt apologized to me this morning," his father said. "He
admitted he was wrong."

"That's simply not good enough," Lockwood said. "He's been
displaying an attitude ever since he got here – his outburst last night
is just the latest. He's damaged our relationships with some of the
locals here."

"Surely the emotional comment of one boy . . . " his mother began.

"You don't understand, Mrs. Brooks. These people have
pride in their country, the same as we do. How would you feel if a
Guyanese came to the United States and proceeded to run down our
country? Rude Americans don't help our cause here, especially ones
that claim to be Christians."

"I'm sorry," Matt said, finally looking up at Lockwood's angry
face. "What do you want me to do, apologize to everyone?"

Lockwood shook his head. "I'd send you home if it were possible. Since it isn't, I want you to stay here at the hotel – out of people's way if at all possible. I can't risk this attitude at the clinic site."

Matt pressed his lips together. "Fine," he said. "I'll stay here." He looked over at his father's laptop which sat on the small desk.

His dad noticed the look. "Oh, no. No privileges. In fact, hand over your iPod and phone."

Matt's head snapped around to look at his father. "What?"

"Mr. Lockwood is right," his father said, his tone more sad than angry. "This is serious, son. I want you to spend the day thinking about what your attitude's been like, not goofing around and glad to get out of work."

"But –" Matt couldn't believe it. "I said I was sorry! Mom, do I have to?"

His mom looked troubled, but said, "I'm not going to go against your father on this, honey. Do what he said."

Matt was stunned. He was being grounded? In Guyana? He shot his father a pleading look, but his dad shook his head and held out his hand. "One day without your electronics won't kill you."

"Fine," Matt muttered. He pulled out his iPod and phone from his pockets and handed them over. "Anything else?"

Steve Lockwood spoke up. "You need to get your act together, kid. I have no problem restricting you to the hotel the rest of your stay here if I have to."

Matt bit back the sarcastic comment that rose to his lips. He understood he was in big trouble at the moment and anything he said would only make it worse.

"Dr. and Mrs. Brooks, we should get going," Lockwood said. "Matt, don't leave the hotel. Try not to cause any more trouble."

Matt followed the adults out of the room. He let his mother briefly hug him before he returned to his own room.

Well, at least he'd get to stay in air conditioning. And he wouldn't have to play kid games. He could just find something to do here at the hotel and stay out of everyone's way.

That was fine with him.

* * *

By the time lunchtime came, Matt thought he would lose his mind.

He'd tried to go swimming. But dark looks from some of the Guyanese there made him feel conspicuous and he found he couldn't enjoy the cool clear water.

He'd thought about confronting one of them, hashing things out. But what good would that do? Besides, he'd probably make things worse and the last thing he wanted to do was give Lockwood another reason to be angry at him.

So Matt found himself back in his room. He'd packed a book from his summer reading list and decided to work on that for a bit. But after a while the words seemed to blur on the page and his head started to throb.

Matt tossed the book towards his suitcase, where it landed on top of some folded pants. At this point, "Duck, Duck, Goose" was starting to look good.

Matt decided he wasn't going to hide out in his room the rest of the day. The people here thought he was an ugly American? Fine, he'd show them they couldn't keep him down. He'd endure their sour looks and prove they couldn't provoke him.

His resolve lasted until he got to the doorway of the dining room. He saw the servers walking around the tables taking orders and realized he didn't have any Guyanese money on him – only American. Would they accept that? Or would his offering it offend them further?

"Hey! You!"

Matt turned and found himself face to face with one of the drivers of the vans. The young man's black eyes narrowed as they glared at Matt. "Why do you hate my country?"

Matt found himself tongue-tied. The guy was taller and beefier than Matt was. He had his fists clenched and Matt knew that in a physical fight this man would beat him to a pulp. "I didn't mean..."

"I heard what you said," the man interrupted. "Why do you hate us?"

"I never said I hated you!" Matt protested. "I don't know you!"

"Do you know Guyana? Tell me why you said that?"

Matt threw his hands up in the air. Fine. If he was going to get creamed, so be it. "I was mad, okay? I didn't want to come here and my parents made me. So I said I hated the place. It was stupid."

The dark-skinned young man stared at Matt for a long moment. Then his face relaxed into a smile. "Yes. It was very stupid."

Matt sighed in relief. It looked like he'd avoided getting killed. "Yeah. Well . . . I'm Matt."

"My name is Anil," the young man answered, shaking Matt's hand. "Would you like to become smarter? We could eat lunch together."

"Um," Matt remembered his worries about eating lunch there. "I don't have any Guyanese money. Just American."

"That's no problem," Anil said. "They take American money here. But today, I will buy you lunch."

"Oh, hey," Matt said. "You don't have to do that."

"I want to," Anil replied. "God has blessed me, I want to pass on His blessings. So I will buy you lunch and we will see what we can learn from each other."

Matt wanted to accept. He looked back into the dining room and took a step inside. Then he remembered the stares he'd been getting. "You might not want to have lunch with me. The servers . . . they're probably still pretty mad at me."

Anil laughed. "They will not stay mad forever. And I promise they will not spit in your food." He threw an arm around Matt's shoulders. "Come on, brother. Let's eat together. Maybe it will help you while you are here."

Out of arguments (and more than a little hungry) Matt let Anil lead him into the dining room.

- TWELVE -

AFTER MATT AND ANIL placed their orders, Matt asked, "So do you like being a driver?"

Anil grinned. "I am driving only this week. I am Steve Lockwood's assistant with People Helping People. Also, I go to the school of preaching here. Someday I will be gospel preacher."

"Oh," Matt said. He felt a little chill when Anil mentioned Steve Lockwood. "Did Lockwood send you to check on me?"

"No, nothing like that," Anil said with a shake of his head. "I prayed about you today and felt a burden on my heart to talk with you. I believe God put it there. That maybe I can help you with whatever is troubling you."

Matt toyed with his water bottle. "I dunno if you'd understand. It'll probably sound stupid to you."

"More stupid then saying you hate Guyana?" Anil asked with a smile. He'd gotten iced tea to drink and now added some of the crystallized sugar to his glass. "I would like to know why you are so unhappy."

Matt sighed. "My folks and I – we just moved to Tampa less than a year ago. I thought it would be cool to live in Florida, you know? Get to go to Disney World, hang out at the beach."

Anil's face lit up. "I've heard of Disney World. Have you ever been there?"

"Not yet," Matt admitted. "I was hoping to go there for our vacation, but then my folks got this idea about going to Guyana. And they insisted I come too."

"So you did not want to be part of the team?" Anil asked.

Matt shook his head. "I'd heard of Guyana – people at the church talked about it – but no, I never wanted to do mission work. Yet here I am."

"And it made you angry."

"Yeah," Matt said. "And –" he stopped talking.

Anil tilted his head. "What else?"

"You won't like it," Matt said. He took a gulp of water, suddenly not wanting to offend this particular Guyanese.

Anil shrugged. "How might you say it? I will not bite you."

Matt laughed. "Thanks." The waitress appeared with their food. Matt waited until she left them alone again. "It's just that it's so hot here – and strange – and I'm covered in bug bites – and it's boring at the site."

He held his breath, waiting for Anil to snap at him and leave the table. Instead, Anil said, "Do you mind if I give thanks for the food?"

Blinking at the change of subject, Matt said, "Sure."

Together they bowed their heads. Anil prayed. "Father, thank you for this food and for all the blessings you have given to us. Thank you for Matt and his fellow Americans coming here. Help him to see my country the way I do, and help him as he tries to do what is right. In Jesus' name, amen."

Matt blinked. "Um, thanks."

"No problem," Anil said, digging into his pork fried rice. "I think that I understand – things are too different for you here."

Matt thought about that as he toyed with his garlic chicken. "Maybe. I'm kinda homesick, you know? I miss my buddies, my Xbox –"

"An Xbox! The 360?" Anil asked.

"Yeah," Matt said. "I have that. A computer too."

"You are rich? Your family?"

Matt shrugged. "I dunno. I guess to some people we are – everyone thinks doctors are rich."

"That is true," Anil agreed. "That was rude of me to ask, I am sorry."

Matt snorted. "You're all right. It didn't bother me."

Anil took a sip of his tea. "I would love to have an Xbox 360 one day. But we don't have electricity in my neighborhood, so there is no point right now."

"What?" Matt couldn't believe what he'd heard. "You don't have electricity?"

"Not yet," Anil said. "For now my parents and my sisters and I make do without it."

"So you don't live in Georgetown?" Matt asked as he sampled his garlic chicken.

"My family lives in a village outside of the city," Anil said. "We have a garden. My father works on a farm and we sell what we grow."

Matt looked at Anil and noticed that his clothing, while clean, was faded. He thought about all the clothes he'd brought from home for the two weeks in Guyana and felt uncomfortable. "Hey, you know, I can pay for lunch…"

Anil shook his head. "Do not worry. Steve pays me well. I have enough for our meal today."

Matt ate some of his fried rice to cover his embarrassment. He'd been griping about how bad the country was and he'd forgotten all that he did have. Anil possessed far less then Matt . . . and he was happy.

Something about that felt wrong.

Anil smiled as he ate. "I tell you what, Matt. Why don't you ask me about Guyana – any question – and I will try to answer it. In return, I will ask you questions about America and you can answer them for me, yes?"

Matt washed down a bite of garlic chicken – he had to admit it was quite tasty – and thought about it. What questions did he have about Guyana? *Was* there anything he wanted to know?

"Does everyone in Guyana drive like a crazy person?" he finally asked.

Anil stared at him for a moment. Then he threw his head back and laughed. "Ah, Matt, that is funny! I remember when Steve first learned to drive here – his driving was so bad, it made me afraid. And I am never afraid on the road."

Matt grinned. "I guess he had to get used to it."

"Yes, yes he did," Anil agreed. "Now he drives like a Guyanese. But at first – oh, Matt, it was something to see."

"So he isn't Mr. Perfect," Matt muttered.

Anil heard him, and a frown appeared on his face. Matt wondered if he'd just ruined everything by one sentence.

"Steve is not perfect," Anil agreed. "Nor am I. Nor are you. We are covered in God's grace, all of us. But Steve is a good man, doing the Lord's work."

"Yeah, I'm sorry," Matt said. "He was just all over me last night and today."

"He cares about the mission. He knows that it is important for the teams that come to make a good impression. A bad one reflects not just on People Helping People, but on the Lord."

"And I'm making a bad impression," Matt sighed.

"Yes, you are," Anil said bluntly. "And it is not helping you, is it? Your attitude does not make you happy, does it?"

Matt sighed. "I guess not."

"I know not," Anil insisted. "You need to find another way to get what you want."

Matt raised an eyebrow. "I've been wanting to go home."

Anil glanced at his watch. "And you will – in twelve days." He pulled out his wallet. "I have work I have to do for Steve. I must go."

"Okay," Matt said. He felt depressed. "Thanks for lunch."

"You are welcome," Anil said, placing some strange colored bills on the table.. "I will tell you one more thing – something you can think about."

"What's that?" Matt asked.

Anil smiled. "You will be here twelve days. Only you can decide if you will be happy or miserable during that time." He waved over the waitress and handed her the money. "I will see you at the devotional tonight, Matt?"

"You'll be there?" Matt asked.

"Tonight I will. You be there too, and tell me what you have decided." Anil got to his feet and with a wink at Matt, left the dining room.

- THIRTEEN -

MATT WENT BACK to his room, thoughts spinning in his head. He took a moment to look around. The maid hadn't come in yet, and the beds were still unmade. His and Robert's suitcases were shoved to the ends of the cots, leaving a narrow pathway across the room to a small balcony.

He pushed open the sliding glass doors and the heat washed over him. Stepping outside he was treated to the view of a several empty rooftops. A small red car drove down the alleyway below him, honking its horn as it spewed exhaust fumes into the humid air..

Matt stood there a long moment, the hot sun beating down on him, and tried to go over lunch again and the things Anil had said. He tried to pace, but the small balcony didn't give him much room to move.

He leaned against the balcony rail. By craning his neck he could see cars on the main street rushing by. Horns punctuated the air, as if there was a law that you had to use your horn every minute or so. People walked by – Matt noticed a tall woman with a basket balanced perfectly on her head stroll down the street.

After a bit he went back into the room. His Bible was buried in his backpack, its battered black cover telling of his casual treatment of the book. He grabbed it and left the room.

For a while he wandered the hotel's halls. Occasionally he ran into one of the maids. He tried smiling and nodding at them. Most of them smiled back. A couple of them frowned – no doubt the tale of the Ugly American had made its rounds to a certain extent.

His meanderings took him to the stairs that led to the roof. He tested the door and found it was unlocked. Pushing it open, he stepped outside.

The chairs for the devotionals were still sitting there. While it was quite warm up on the roof, a breeze made it almost bearable. Matt felt his head clear to a certain extent. He felt as if he'd found his place to think.

Georgetown – at least the part visible to him from here – spread out before him. Matt leaned against the parapet and took stock of the city. It didn't look as clean or polished as Tampa. The buildings were shorter – in fact, the Phoenix appeared to be the tallest building in the area. Far below he saw cars wending their way through traffic, along with several horse-drawn carts.

Matt fingered his Bible. He was an average student of the Word, able to keep up with his Bible class teacher and okay in memorizing verses.

He'd been baptized when he was fourteen. After his initial excitement of becoming a Christian – for days he couldn't get enough of the Bible – he'd settled down to what he came to think of was the norm. Which was not all that different from how he'd been living before he'd chosen to become a Christian.

Looking down at the worn cover with his name in gold on the lower right corner, he tried to remember the last time he'd cracked the book open. He'd taken to using his Bible program on his phone when at church and stuff. And he hadn't been doing a lot of reading on his own.

Matt recalled his mother's favorite passage – Romans 8:28. He turned to it, fumbling with the thin pages.

"And we know that all things work together for good to them that love God, to them who are the called according to His purpose," he read.

Matt stared at the statement. "All things – " well, that was pretty direct, wasn't it? "All" didn't leave anything out, did it?

"Work together for good." But what was good? He had to admit his attitude wasn't all that great. But how could anything good come from this trip?

"To them that love God." He loved God, didn't he? He prayed, went to church, watched his language. He didn't steal, or kill people, he didn't fool around with girls – didn't that all mean he loved God?

"to them who are the called according to His purpose." Did God have a purpose for Matt being in Guyana?

Matt let his head droop for a moment. He remembered one of the last things Anil had said – that it was his choice whether to be happy or miserable over the rest of his time here.

Was it that simple? He pulled his bottle of water from his waistpack and took a long drink. Could he choose his way out of the dark cloud that had hung over him ever since he'd started his trip here?

He didn't think he could do it. Not by himself.

His eyes dropped down to his Bible. But did he have to do it by himself?

He clasped his hands on top of the open book. Looked up at the clear blue sky. Softly he began to pray.

"God, I want to do what's right. I say I love You, but I want to show it better. Please change my attitude. Make me want to be here. You say everything works to the good for those that love You. Show me how this is good. Help me to be a better person. Thanks. In Jesus name, amen."

He dropped his head back down and gazed at the street far below. He waited.

Nothing happened.

No great flashes of insight. And he still didn't want to be here. He still felt hot, his arms still itched from the bug bites, and he was still mad that he'd been brought here in the first place.

Why didn't God change any of that?

Matt resisted the sudden urge he had to toss his Bible off the roof. He headed back to the door that led downstairs. What was he going to do?

He gave the door a yank. Nothing happened.

Concerned, he twisted the knob and pulled again. The door refused to open.

Had someone come along and locked the door? That would be perfect, wouldn't it? He'd be stuck up here for hours and no one would know where he was and Lockwood would probably yell at him again.

He jiggled the knob hard and noticed it was a little loose in the door. Maybe it wasn't locked, maybe it was just stuck.

He spent a good five minutes twisting the knob, shaking it, trying to get the door open. Sweat poured down his face. He couldn't be stuck up here. He *couldn't*.

Finally the door popped open. Matt dove into the relative coolness of the stairwell. His heart began to slow as he realized he was okay, the door was just tricky.

He made a mental note to make mention of the fact at tonight's devotional and headed back to his room, relieved and discouraged.

* * *

As he'd promised, Anil was at the devotional that night. Lockwood was there too – in fact, he led it.

Matt sat in the back again, feeling isolated. His parents were the only ones who'd talked to him since everyone came back from the clinic site that day.

His mom told him that one of the people she'd studied with was baptized. His father mentioned that he and the other doctors had seen over four hundred patients. The room buzzed with excitement.

Matt felt apart from it all. Worse, he knew he had no one but himself to blame for that feeling.

Lockwood praised the group for the work they'd done so far. "I know it's hot and you're probably tired, but believe me, you're making a difference here. I appreciate your service and the Guyanese people do as well."

Matt sat for a moment after the group was dismissed. He saw Anil and Steve talking off to the side. Anil caught Matt's eye and raised an inquiring eyebrow.

Matt realized there was one decision he could make. He got up and walked to where the two men stood. "Excuse me? Mr. Lockwood?"

Lockwood frowned. "What is it, Matt?"

It wasn't easy. Matt swallowed and said, "I want another chance."

Lockwood studied him. "I'm not sure about that. I can't afford you to blow up on the site like you did here. I've already spent part of today doing damage control."

"Yes, sir," Matt said, fighting the urge to say forget it and go back to his room. "I promise you I won't go off like that again. Please, let me go back to the site tomorrow."

"Steve? I may say something?" Anil said.

"What?"

"I had lunch with Matt today," Anil told the missionary. "He admits what he said was stupid. I think he wants to make things right. You should give him another chance."

"Really?" Lockwood said.

"Yes, really," Anil nodded. "I think he's decided he wants to change. We should give him the opportunity to do so."

Lockwood pulled on his beard as he thought. Then he turned to Matt. "Okay. One chance. Blow this, kid, and you'll spend the rest of the trip locked in your room. Do I make myself clear?"

Matt nodded. "Yeah. Thanks."

Anil grinned at him. "See you tomorrow – you ride with me, up front, okay? We can talk then."

"Okay," Matt said. He headed back to his room, feeling slightly better.

He had another chance.

He hoped God would help him make something of it.

- FOURTEEN -

MATT GOT OUT OF BED the next morning as Robert was leaving the bathroom, rubbing a towel through his hair. "Morning, Robert."

"Morning," Robert replied. He said nothing else as he picked up a pale yellow dress shirt and began to put it on.

Matt paused on his way to the bathroom. The two of them hadn't spoken very much at all the night before, and Robert didn't seem welcoming of conversation at the moment.

Still, Matt felt the need to say something, to reestablish lines of communications his attitude had broken. So he leaned against the doorway to the restroom and said, "Can I ask you something?"

A look of surprise crossed Robert's face. His fingers paused in their job of buttoning his shirt. "Okay."

"This isn't the first time you've come to Guyana?" Matt asked.

Robert tilted his head as he thought. "This is my second – no, make that my third – time. I came over with my mom when I was fifteen."

Matt nodded. Then before he lost his nerve, he asked, "Do you like it here?"

He expected the other teenager to say of course he liked it in Guyana, so he was surprised when Robert seemed to mull over his answer. "I don't hate it, if that's what you're asking."

Matt winced at his roommate's words. "I shouldn't have said that."

Robert shrugged. "I don't mind coming here, but would I move here to live? No. I like Tampa a whole lot better."

Matt frowned. "You don't seem to mind it."

"I don't go around complaining about things," Robert said. "But do I like sitting outside in tropical weather and eating cold food out of a can for lunch? Not my favorite ways to pass the time."

Matt didn't know what to say for a moment. He looked down at his bare feet. "I know what you mean," he muttered.

There was a brief silence. Matt turned to go into the bathroom when Robert spoke up. "Hey Matt?"

"Yeah?"

"It helps to focus on the good stuff. It makes the rest of it seem not so bad."

Matt considered that. "Okay. Thanks."

"No problem," Robert said. "But you'd better hurry and get ready if you want some breakfast."

Matt quickly went into the bathroom to start his morning routine. While showering, he tried to think of something good to focus on while in Guyana.

Nothing came to mind.

This wasn't going to be easy.

* * *

"Matt!" Anil called. The Guyanese man stood next to the second van in line, a broad smile on his face. "Come on, I saved your seat."

Matt hurried over, his parents behind him. "Thanks," he said as Anil opened the door for him with a flourish.

"It is no problem," Anil told him. "These are your parents?"

"Yeah," Matt made quick introductions.

Anil clasped Matt's dad's hands. "I am grateful for you coming to my country to help us out. Your medical care . . . you have no idea how many lives you touch."

"Thank you," Matt's dad said. He and his wife climbed into the van to sit in the middle seat.

Matt felt weird sitting in front. At home, he'd have the steering wheel and dashboard in front of him. It still felt wrong to see them on the right-hand side of the car.

A few minutes later Anil swung into the driver's seat. "Here we go!" he told Matt cheerfully. "You've got a good view to see Guyanese traffic, yes?"

"Yeah," Matt said, trying to sound confident. He put on his seatbelt without being asked, grateful that at least the front seats possessed them.

Moments later he was trying not to be obvious as he clutched at his seat. Anil wove through traffic, missing cars in front of him by what looked like inches to Matt.

"You drive yet, Matt?" Anil asked as he swerved around a slower moving vehicle, leaning on his horn as he did so.

"Nope," Matt gulped. He was braced for the sound of metal against metal as Anil swung back into his original lane.

Anil laughed. "From what you tell me, traffic in America is more sedate?"

Matt thought of the I-4/I-275 interchange near downtown Tampa and how much his dad hated driving through there in rush hour. "Mostly," he told Anil.

"I bet I would be a good driver in America," Anil told Matt.

Matt didn't know how to answer that, so he just held his seat a little more tightly. He couldn't repress a sigh of relief when they finally arrived at the clinic site.

Before he got out of the car, Anil caught his eye. "You make good decisions today. Later we will talk about them, okay?"

Matt nodded. "I'll try."

"Trust in the Lord, brother, and in His power," Anil said before getting out of the van and opening up the side doors.

"When did you meet Anil, honey?" his mother asked as the crossed the planks that were laid over the drainage ditch.

"Yesterday at lunch," Matt said. "He seems like an okay guy."

"That he does," his dad said from behind them. "Be polite with him, Matt. I'd rather we got along with the people here."

Matt felt his face redden. "Yes, sir," he replied. He touched the phone in his pocket – his parents had returned his electronics the night before. "Thanks again for giving my stuff back."

"Just don't give me a reason to take them again," his father warned before heading inside.

Matt felt frustrated. He was willing to try, wasn't he? Why was his dad on his case like this?

His mother put a hand on his shoulder. "He's tired, Matt. I know you think he's being hard on you, but you really hurt him the other night."

Matt's shoulders slumped. "I said I was sorry."

"We know," his mother said. "But sometimes things hurt even if you're sorry for them. Just try to do better and your dad will see that and lighten up."

Matt stuck his hands in his pockets. He looked over to where the Bible studies were being conducted and noticed a long ladder going up to the roof. "What's going on over there?"

"Stan decided we could finish the roof for them while we were here," his mom replied. "Several of the young men have lent a hand – you could probably help too."

Matt frowned. "They're doing that while you're doing Bible studies? How do you handle the noise?"

"We talk very loudly," his mom said with a grin. "Yes, it's difficult but we're managing. And it will help the congregation here if we finish the room off."

Matt wiped the sweat off his face as he looked at the roof. Jenna walked by, chatting with Susie. He lowered his gaze. "Hey Jenna, Susie."

Susie greeted him. Jenna gave no sign of having heard him.

Matt felt discouraged as he watched the two of them go into the building. Jenna was still mad at him? That sucked.

"Do better," everyone kept telling him.

But what if he didn't know how?

- FIFTEEN -

MATT HAMMERED DOWN another roof shingle. He carefully put down his hammer in front of him and pulled out his water bottle.

He wasn't just hot. Working on the roof made him feel grimy as well. He took a long drink of water and looked over his progress so far. About half of the roof was shingled now.

Chuck looked up from where he was also placing shingles. "Hey Matt, have you had a break yet?"

"I'm good," Matt said. He frowned at his now empty water bottle. He thought he'd just filled the thing a short time before.

Chuck shook his head. "Go get some more water. Dehydration isn't fun here. You don't want them to hook you up to an IV."

Matt couldn't argue with that statement. He eased himself over to where the ladder stood and climbed down to the ground.

He could see right into the Bible study area. There was a murmur of voices as about a dozen pairs of people talked together. He saw his mom and gave her a quick wave that she returned before turning back to the woman she was speaking with, her gaze intense.

Matt headed to the break room. His backpack was here and he took a moment to pull out an energy bar he'd brought for a snack. The heat meant the bar was half-melted in the wrapper but Matt devoured it anyway, washing it down with half a bottle's worth of Gatorade.

He refilled his water bottle and sat on one of the benches He was surprised to have the room to himself at the moment – usually there were one or two others taking a brief break from whatever they were doing. At the same time he felt glad to be alone, just for a minute.

It was hard, but he was trying. He'd thought about the things Anil and Robert had said to him and had racked his brain to come up with things to be thankful for in Guyana. The only thing he'd come up with so far today was that at least it hadn't rained while he was on the roof, and that just wasn't a positive enough thought to focus on.

Stan stuck his head in the doorway. "Hey, Matt. You doing all right?"

Matt nodded. "Yeah. Just taking a break before I go back on the roof."

Stan came inside the room and looked at Matt's arms. Under a number of mosquito bites the skin was pink. "Looks like you're getting a lot of sun up there. Did you use sunscreen?"

Matt glanced down at his arms, surprised. "I didn't think about it," he admitted. "I don't even know if we brought any."

"I'm sure your folks did," Stan said. "In the meantime, how about giving a hand with the kids again after your break? You can relieve one of the girls. We've had a lot of kids today and the three of them have been working hard to keep them occupied."

"I can go back on the roof," Matt protested. He didn't say that he didn't want to work with the kids, though he certainly thought it!

"I know you can but I need you with the kids more at the moment," Stan said. "I'm cycling through you guys so you take turns up there – and I'm not lacking for workers."

"Fine," Matt sighed.

Stan frowned. "Look, it might not be your favorite thing, but looking after the young ones is important too. It frees the parents up for Bible study – and if the kids have a positive experience, their folks tend to like that."

"I said I would," Matt answered. He knew he sounded grumpy and he felt badly. Why hadn't God changed his heart? Why was he still feeling this way?

Before Stan could reply two older women came into the break room. Stan greeted them and then looked at Matt. "Don't take too long," he said.

Matt said nothing, just sipped his water and listened to the two women. One was teaching basic first aid to some of the Guyanese, while the other was one of the nurses. They chattered about people Matt didn't know while they pulled out their cold lunches.

Soon after they started eating, Matt got up and went back outside. He saw where the kids were playing another game of "Duck, Duck, Goose" and with an inward sigh went over to where the group was gathered.

He saw Jenna glance at him and then look away. That irritated him. Weren't Christians supposed to be forgiving?

He spoke to Nancy. "Stan sent me over so one of you could take a break."

"Oh, that's great, thanks," Nancy said. She looked over at Jenna who was now cheering the kids on in their game. "Hey Jenna? Susie? I'm going to go to the break room. You've got Matt here to take my place."

"That's great," said Susie. "Hey Matt, why don't you come play for a while? Then maybe we can sing some songs."

"Sure," Matt said. He moved to sit on the hard ground next to a young boy who was pouting. The boy, who wore a faded Power Rangers t-shirt and some ragged shorts, sat with his arms folded over his knees. He seemed fascinated with his bare toes.

"Okay, let's go," Jenna said. "Timmy, you're it."

Matt waited. Sure enough, he got picked by Timmy and ran slowly around the circle so that the lad got to where Matt had been sitting. That made Matt "it."

He wondered why the child he'd been sitting next to was pouting. Most of the kids seemed pretty happy, so what was his problem? Matt thought about it while he slowly went around the circle, touching each child on the head as he said, "Duck…"

When he got to the little boy in the Power Rangers t-shirt, he touched his head and quickly said, "Goose!" He started around the circle while the other kids yelled at the one he'd picked to get up and give chase.

Matt got halfway around the circle before he realized he wasn't being pursued. The little boy sat where he was, now hugging his knees to his chest.

Jenna was at the child's side in an instant, her expression concerned as she talked to the child in low tones. The child shook his head at something she said that Matt couldn't catch.

Finally Jenna led the child out of the circle. "You'll have to pick someone else," she said. "Barry doesn't feel like playing right now."

Well, neither do I, thought Matt. But he knew that unlike Barry, he didn't have a choice.

Wondering what was going on with Barry, Matt started around the circle again. "Duck . . . duck . . . "

* * *

After the gospel meeting that night, Matt found himself looking for a kid wearing a Power Rangers t-shirt. He told himself it was none of his business why the child was unhappy. But he discovered that his curiosity was piqued.

He could have asked Jenna. But Matt had trouble talking with Jenna when she *wasn't* mad at him. Now that she was, he didn't know how to start a conversation.

He found the little boy clutching the hand of a woman who was dressed in an orange wraparound dress. She was talking to Jenna. The child was staring at the floor, not running around like the other kids.

Matt came up and heard the woman say, ". . . it be hard for our family right now. My husband, he go out today to the mines. He will be there a long time. This one," she gestured to Barry, "he miss his daddy. But we need the money."

Matt crouched down. He could kind of understand the kid's feelings. When he'd been this kid's age – around seven or eight, he guessed – Matt had hated it when his dad had to go on trips.

He glanced up at the mother. "How long will his dad be gone?" he asked.

"A month," she answered. Jenna glanced at him, her face a mixture of anger and surprise.

Matt ignored her. He looked at the frowning kid. "Hey, I know that's no fun."

The kid didn't respond. Matt remembered something his mom used to do to him when he was sulking. He decided to try it.

"Okay then," he said. "Don't smile."

The boy flicked his gaze up at Matt, then looked back down at his feet.

"I mean it," Matt continued. "Don't smile. No grinning or giggling either, no matter what. Even if you think about pink elephants."

The boy's mouth twitched.

"Didn't you hear me?" Matt said. "No smiling. I don't want to see those teeth of yours, even if I cross my eyes like this…" he trailed off as the boy looked up at him, his mouth twitching again.

"Uh-oh, what's going on?" he asked. "What am I seeing here? I said no smiles! What are you doing?"

A tiny giggle escaped as the boy's lips curved upwards. He glanced at Matt and giggled again when Matt crossed his eyes a second time.

Matt grinned. He heard Barry's mother's low laughter and looked up at her with a smile. He then caught Jenna looking at him and shrugged, his smile faltering just a little bit.

She looked at him, and then slowly gave a small smile in return.

Matt stood up and rubbed Barry's curly head. He still didn't want to be here. He knew his attitude still stank.

But making a sad little boy laugh? That didn't feel bad at all.

- SIXTEEN -

THE NEXT DAY PASSED slowly for Matt. His feelings at cheering up Barry the night before were gone by the time he'd awakened. He'd been assigned to working with the kids again, which was both good and bad. Bad because no matter how hard he tried, he was bored out of his mind.

Good, because at least now Jenna was talking to him. She said "Good morning" to him when she got in the van he was riding in (Matt was once again seated in the front at Anil's insistence). She acted friendlier when they were with the kids too, smiling as he took their pictures and made funny faces.

Matt brooded over things on the ride back. Everyone said he could choose how he felt about things. He'd prayed again, when he got up that morning, for God to change his attitude.

So why was he still unhappy? Why did he want to do nothing more than complain about being in Guyana? And why was he still so homesick?

Anil, sensing his mood, didn't speak to him during the drive. However, when they got to the hotel, he stopped Matt from leaving the van. "Just a minute, Matt. I want to talk with you."

Matt sighed and rested his head back against the taped up seat. Anil quickly let everyone else out of the van, then climbed back into the driver's seat. "What's wrong, man? Your face is longer than my arm."

Matt frowned. "I'm trying, Anil, okay? I've been praying about it and I really want to have a better attitude about everything."

"And you do not," Anil said.

"Nope, I don't," Matt said. "God isn't doing anything to change me. I still don't want to be here, I still miss home."

Anil shrugged. "God is not going to just snap His fingers and change your mind or your heart, Matt. You must decide to change."

"But I did decide," Matt argued. "I really don't want to be unhappy the rest of my time here, but I just can't seem to kick out this mood."

Anil cocked his head. "Have you signed up for a Saturday trip yet?"

Matt remembered that the group had Saturday off. Lockwood had mentioned a number of day trips that were being offered for those who were interested.

"I haven't," he told Anil. "I figured I'd just hang around the hotel."

"No, you must not do that," Anil said. "I am taking a group to the Kaieteur National Park. There are wondrous things there. Perhaps you can find an answer to your attitude in God's creation."

Matt thought about it. He remember how cooped up he'd felt in the hotel on Tuesday. Maybe a trip to a park wasn't such a bad idea. And he'd have more time to spend with Anil, whom he discovered he was growing to like more and more.

"Okay," he said. "I'll sign up if my folks are okay with it."

"Wonderful!" Anil said. He made shooing motions with his hands. "Time for you to go eat dinner. Tomorrow you ride with me again, yes? And I will pray to God for your attitude."

"Thanks," Matt said, sliding out of the van. He hurried into the dining room, not wanting to miss out on dinner.

* * *

Matt's parents agreed on his taking the trip to the national park, signing up for it themselves. "It'll be good to see more of the country," his dad said. "After this week, a little peaceful sightseeing without being Dr. Brooks sounds perfect."

Matt glanced at his father. There were shadows under his eyes and he yawned. Matt remembered that the doctors were seeing a lot of patients – it was only Thursday and the total number of patients seen was around a thousand for the week. No wonder he was ready for a break.

Matt checked out his dinner. They'd had spaghetti with sauce on the buffet, and he carefully sampled it. To his surprise, the flavor of the sauce was more like barbeque. He put his fork down with a grimace.

"Everything all right?" his mother asked.

"It . . . the sauce tastes strange," Matt said. He nibbled at a meatball and was relieved that it tasted normal.

His mother sampled her own portion and her eyebrows went up. "You're not kidding. This isn't like any marinara I've had." She met Matt's eyes and smiled. "We're just having to get used to a lot of different things on this trip."

Matt went back to studying his plate. He didn't want to say what he was thinking, which was that he was tired of things that were different.

He wanted to go home.

* * *

"Hey Matt?" Robert asked as the two teenagers were getting ready for bed.

"Yeah?" Matt said, examining his leg where one of the kids had kicked him that day. It had been an accident, but it still hurt.

"Don't take this wrong, but do you like working with the kids?"

Matt looked up at where Robert stood, his red plaid dress shirt in his hands. Robert looked wary, as if he were unsure of Matt's reaction.

Matt tossed his pants into his suitcase. "Honestly? It's boring." He frowned. "Is it that obvious?"

Robert hung his shirt up in the small closet they shared. "Yes and no. I mean, you don't act very happy, and I was wondering if getting stuck with the kids was part of it."

Matt tensed. Righteous Robert was asking questions Matt wasn't sure he wanted to answer. Confiding in Anil was one thing – but Robert? Mr. Perfect Preacher's Kid?

Robert's cheeks flushed. "Okay, I guess I'm out of line. I was just going to ask you . . . no, forget it."

"What?" Matt asked, curious in spite of himself.

"Well," Robert said, sliding out of his shoes, "I was thinking – you're okay with Bible stuff, I see you in class, you seem to do okay, right?"

"Yeah. So?"

"So," Robert took a deep breath, "I wondered if you wanted to sit in on some of my Bible studies tomorrow? For something else to do. It might be more interesting to you."

"Why are you asking me this?" Matt asked, surprised.

Robert looked down at his hands, clasped in his lap. "Well, in the devo tonight, remember how Chuck talked about how Jesus went around and helped people, and we're to follow that example?"

"Yeah," Matt said.

"I got to thinking," Robert continued, "that I'm all about helping the Guyanese people, but haven't tried to lend a hand to my own roommate." Robert bit his lip. "I mean, I'm not trying to put you down, but you seem to be having a rough time of it. I just thought I could help."

Matt stared at Robert. He'd not exactly been nice to the teen – yeah, he'd opened up a little bit more to him the past couple of days but he hadn't stopped thinking badly about him. And here the guy was, trying to help him out.

"Well," he said, thinking it out as he spoke, "do you think Stan would go for it? If so, sure, I'll sit with you."

A quick grin flashed across Robert's face. "Yeah? That's great. I'll talk to Stan, I bet he'll be okay with it."

Matt nodded. "Thanks."

"No problem," Robert answered.

Matt swung his legs into the cot and pulled the sheet up. He turned off his light and faced the wall. "Good night," he said.

"Night," Robert answered. A few minutes later his light was out.

Matt lay there thinking. He'd just agreed to sit in on Bible studies. That was probably going to be boring as well. After all, he bet he knew all the Scriptures Robert would use.

But then again, it wasn't "Duck, Duck, Goose."

- SEVENTEEN -

W HEN MATT CAME into the dining room the next morning, he saw Robert already talking to Stan. They were both seated at a table along with Dr. Lopez and his wife.

As Matt piled pancakes on his plate, he wondered what Stan would say. For that matter, would Steve Lockwood have an opinion? Had Matt messed things up so thoroughly that he wasn't going to be trusted?

He saw his folks sitting with another couple. His mom saw him looking their way. "Come on, Matt, pull up a chair."

Matt glanced around until he saw an empty chair where Chuck and Brad were sitting. "Can I take this?" he asked them.

"Sure," Chuck said with a shrug. Matt dragged the chair to where his folks sat and put his plate down. He was headed to the coffeemaker when Stan called his name.

This was it. Matt resolved that he'd show no reaction if Stan said no. Maybe it was God's will that he spend the trip going out of his mind. Why God would punish him like that, he wasn't sure.

Stan stood up, as did Robert. The older man was frowning. "Robert says you'd like to sit in on some Bible studies with him today."

"Yes sir," Matt said, keeping his eyes on Stan's blue ones.

Stan stroked his mustache. "I can't afford having you blow up at someone. You think you can keep it under control?"

Matt felt annoyed. He thought about telling Stan to forget it and going back to his breakfast. Before he could, Robert spoke up. "He only did it once, Stan, and he apologized for it. He hasn't gone off on anyone else all week."

Great. Now Righteous Robert was defending him. This was getting better and better.

"I'll mention it to Steve," Stan said finally. "Go back and eat, Matt. I'll let you know my decision when we get to the site."

"Fine," Matt said. He turned and went to get some coffee, trying to tamp down his anger. Mention it to Lockwood? Matt was pretty sure what *he* would have to say about it. He might as well forget about it.

He dropped down in his chair and began to eat his breakfast. "Everything all right, honey?" his mom asked.

Matt swallowed a mouthful of pancake. "Yeah," he said. It wasn't but there was no point in ruining her day, too.

Matt tuned out the adults' conversation and thought about the situation. *God, what else can I do? No one will even give me a chance!*

Trust in the LORD with all thine heart; and lean not unto thine own understanding.

Matt blinked. Huh? Where'd that come from? He remembered it was a passage in Proverbs somewhere. He pulled out his phone and did a quick search in his Bible program, and discovered it was the fifth verse in the third chapter.

His eyes traveled down to the verse following it: *In all thy ways acknowledge him, and he shall direct thy paths.*

Matt took a sip of coffee while he contemplated the verse. God would direct his paths, eh? Did that mean God made him come to Guyana? Would God decide what he'd do while he was here?

He decided a quick prayer couldn't hurt. *God, I know I still have an attitude problem. But could You please get someone to give me a chance here? I do want to change, I just don't know how. Help me make it happen, okay? In Jesus' name, amen.*

Matt took another bite of syrup-soaked pancake. He didn't feel any different. But maybe now the ball was in God's court. Maybe He'd do something that would change things for Matt, finally.

Maybe.

* * *

It took a lot of self-control but Matt did not go up to where Stan and Steve stood, talking. He saw Steve glance his way once and knew the conversation was about him.

Anil called to him. "Come on! Get into the van! Hurry up!"

Matt climbed into the front seat again. Anil grinned at him. "So how are you feeling today? Any better?"

"I dunno," Matt said. "I prayed about it at breakfast this morning. I'm hoping I can sit in on some of the Bible studies."

"That would be a good thing," Anil said. "Teaching people the Good News is always good."

"I bet Lockwood says no," Matt griped. "I bet he doesn't trust me."

"Do not say that about Steve," Anil chided him. "If he did not trust you, you would not be going to the site."

"I guess," Matt said. He stared out the window and saw the two men finish up their conversation. Matt tried to guess what the decision was from looking at Stan's face but the older man's expression gave nothing away as he hurried to one of the other vans.

A few minutes later they were off bouncing down the street. Potholes were frequent, and once you got outside of Georgetown, not all the roads were paved. Sometimes Anil had to slow down to maneuver around a washed out section of road.

Anil did his best to miss the worst parts of the roads, but it wasn't always possible. Matt yelped after a particularly hard jounce. "You okay over there?" Anil asked.

"Yeah," Matt said. He vowed to never complain about the road conditions in Tampa again.

They got to the clinic and Matt went to drop off his backpack in the break room. Stan stopped him before he could enter the building. "Hang on there, Matt."

"Yeah?" Matt said, gripping the strap of his backpack tightly.

"I talked to Steve. We decided to go ahead and let you sit in on the Bible studies with Robert today," Stan said.

"You did?" Matt tried and failed to hide the surprise in his voice. He wondered if he'd heard wrong.

Stan nodded. "Steve said it would be okay, as long as someone was with you. I trust Robert, so we'll give it a try."

"Um, thanks," Matt said. He'd been so prepared for a "no" that the "yes" answer stunned him.

Stan nodded. "Hang on to your backpack. We're asking those doing the studies to keep their stuff with them, to allow more room for other people's gear. Okay?"

"Yeah, fine," Matt said. He watched as Stan rushed off to catch someone else coming off the vans. *Well what do you know. Maybe God is answering one of my prayers.*

With that thought in mind, Matt went to find Robert and tell him the news.

* * *

"So do you understand God's plan of salvation?" Robert asked the thin Guyanese man sitting next to him. Matt sat on the teen's other side, his Bible open in his lap.

The man nodded. "Yes, I do."

"Then are you ready to obey the gospel?" Robert asked.

Matt found himself holding his breath. Maybe this time . . .

The older man shook his head. "No, I am not."

Matt felt disappointment sweep over him. Another no!

In contrast, Robert appeared calm and interested. "May I ask why not, sir?"

"I am not ready," the man said simply. He shifted a little in his chair. "My whole family is Hindu. I am Hindu. I am not ready to go against my family."

Matt sighed.

Robert spoke with the man for a few more minutes, then finally said, "Well, I'm sorry to hear this. The church is here if you should change your mind."

Matt's shoulders slumped as Robert signed the man's intake paper. This had been the third "no" in a row.

Matt was no longer bored – he was discouraged.

The studies themselves had proven interesting. While Matt was familiar with the scriptures Robert used, he'd never seen them put together in this way. The study, encased in a black three-ring binder, took a person step by step through God's word and the plan of salvation laid out there.

Robert himself proved to be a patient teacher, and had come up with analogies that reinforced what the Bible was teaching. And he did it with a cheerful attitude that persisted in spite of all the rejections.

Matt wondered how he did it. When they took their lunch break, he asked.

Robert said, "I look at it this way – I'm just the messenger. It's up to them to accept or reject it."

Matt chewed on room temperature canned spaghetti and meatballs – even cold it tasted better than the sauce they'd had the night before. "I don't get it."

Robert put down the can of deviled ham he was consuming and picked up his Bible. "You ever read Ezekiel?"

"You mean on purpose?" Matt asked.

Robert laughed. "Yeah, some of it is pretty strange. But there's a cool passage about being a watchman in chapter 33." He flipped over to that part of the Bible and began to read:

"Again the word of the LORD came unto me, saying, Son of man, speak to the children of thy people, and say unto them, When I bring the sword upon a land, if the people of the land take a man of their coasts, and set him for their watchman: If when he seeth the sword come upon the land, he blow the trumpet, and warn the people; Then whosoever heareth the sound of the trumpet, and taketh not warning; if the sword come, and take him away, his blood shall be upon his own head. He heard the sound of the trumpet, and took not warning; his blood shall be upon him. But he that taketh warning shall deliver his soul.

"But if the watchman see the sword come, and blow not the trumpet, and the people be not warned; if the sword come, and take any person from among them, he is taken away in his iniquity; but his blood will I require at the watchman's hand.

"So thou, O son of man, I have set thee a watchman unto the house of Israel; therefore thou shalt hear the word at my mouth, and warn them from me. Nevertheless, if thou warn the wicked of his way to turn from it; if he do not turn from his way, he shall die in his iniquity; but thou hast delivered thy soul."

Matt frowned. "So God was saying that if Ezekiel didn't warn people about their sins God would hold him responsible?"

Something like that," Robert said. "But he also says that if Ezekiel warned a wicked man to change and he didn't, God didn't blame Ezekiel for his choice. I figure as long as I share the message, I'm being the watchman."

Matt thought for a moment. "I haven't been sharing my faith. I guess I'm a lousy watchman."

Robert took a sip of water. "The good thing is you can change that if you want to. Tell you what – watch me some more, and then you can try conducting a Bible study. Sound good?"

"Me?" Matt squeaked. "But I've never done it before!"

"I'll be right there to help," Robert said. "Come on, you can do it."

Matt swallowed the dryness in his throat. *Conduct a Bible study? Could he do it?*

- EIGHTEEN -

MATT WATCHED ROBERT as the teen conducted several more studies. As he observed and fumbled for the verses Robert cited, Matt realized he was sweating – and it wasn't just because it was hot.

Well, you can't say you're bored now, he thought as Robert concluded another study with another person saying "no" to the invitation to become a Christian. Nope, instead of bored he was flirting with terrified.

Robert took a swig of water. "Well? You ready to give it a try?"

Matt tried to control his panic. "Let me watch you one more time, okay?"

"Sure, no pressure, Matt," Robert said. "If you're not up for it, it's not a big deal, okay?"

But it was a big deal, at least to Matt. He kept thinking about the verses Robert had read from Ezekiel. He turned back to that part of the Bible, reading it over again.

When I say unto the wicked, O wicked man, thou shalt surely die; if thou dost not speak to warn the wicked from his way, that wicked man shall die in his iniquity; but his blood will I require at thine hand.

Matt felt as if the words were weights on his shoulders. God had taken warning Israel very seriously. Didn't it stand to reason that he felt the same way about warning people who weren't Christians?

He'd never really thought about it before this. Now, Matt wondered how God felt about him and his really not trying to share his faith.

Robert was greeting a tired-looking young lady who had a baby perched on her hip. They sat down and Robert began to go through the study with her, taking his time.

Matt was grateful for Robert's patience just then. He craned his neck to read the study book Robert had. When the teen mentioned a Scripture Matt worked to flip to it. He found after sitting through several studies it was becoming easier to find the verses in question.

When Robert concluded the study and asked the woman if she was willing to make a commitment, she looked down at her baby for a moment. Then, in a soft voice, she said, "Yes. I would like to obey the gospel."

Matt's mouth dropped open. He'd fully expected another "no." The fact she said yes . . . he felt excitement run through him.

Robert was grinning. He stood up at waved at Harry, who was talking to Stan in the doorway. Harry came over and Robert repeated what the young woman had said.

With a broad smile, Harry took the woman by the hand. "God bless you, sister, for making such a choice. Come with me and we'll get you ready. We have some clothes you can change into so yours stay dry."

"Come on," Robert said. "Have you seen a baptism here?"

Matt shook his head. "Where do they baptize people?" he asked. There was no baptistry in the building and Matt didn't think there was a river nearby.

Robert grinned. "You'll see."

Matt followed Robert to the rear of the building. Some of the local men and women who were helping out with the clinic were gathering together. Matt saw an older Guyanese woman leading the young lady to the outhouse.

Robert pointed to where the locals were gathered. "Look."

Matt stared. There was a large barrel sitting on the grass, filled with water. A short stepladder was pushed against it. "That's their baptistry?"

"Isn't it amazing?" Robert asked.

Matt scratched his head. He'd never thought of using a barrel to baptize someone. He guessed you did what you had to.

A few drops of rain spattered down but no one left the area. Matt saw the young woman come out of the outhouse, dressed in an old pair of shorts and a dark blue t-shirt. Harry and Stan helped her up the steps and lowered her into the barrel. Matt saw Harry's wife Carmen standing in the crowd. She was holding the baby, who cooed and played with her beaded necklace.

Harry spoke to the woman quietly for a moment, then asked her to state her confession to all. Matt strained to hear her say, "Jesus is Lord."

"God bless you for that confession," the Guyanese preacher said. "I now baptize you in the name of the Father, and of the Son, and of the Holy Spirit, for the forgiveness of your sins."

What that he gently submerged her into the water. When he pulled her out, several of the men called out, "Amen!"

Matt saw her smile back at Harry as he helped her out of the barrel. Once she was out Carmen handed back the baby and everyone made a circle around their new sister in Christ. Stan asked Robert to lead them in a prayer for her.

As Robert prayed, Matt discovered he couldn't stop grinning. He'd seen baptisms before, and he remembered his own several years ago. But he'd never seen someone studied with like he had today and seen them accept the truth.

All of a sudden Matt *wanted* to conduct a study. He wanted to lead someone to that point, see them become a child of God. He wanted to try.

"Wasn't that great?" Robert said, clapping Matt on the shoulder as the two ran back under the roof – the spattering of rain was becoming a downpour.

"Yeah," Matt said. "I bet you feel pumped after that."

Robert smiled. "Yeah, it feels pretty good. But it's God working through me. Can't forget that."

"I want that," Matt said. "I want to try and do a study. You think I can?"

"Sure do," Robert said. He handed Matt the study guide. "Here. Take another look at it real fast, before Stan sends us someone else."

Matt scanned the study, suddenly nervous. He wanted to do this, sure, but what if he screwed it up? This was important, wasn't it? Wasn't that part of the point of Ezekiel 33, that giving God's message to someone was important?

"Here we go," Robert said. "Don't worry. I'll help you if you need it."

Matt got up and awkwardly shook hands with the woman who came up to him. She was large, wearing a tight floral print dress. The chair she sat in creaked.

Matt introduced himself and found out her name was Melinda. He went through his questions and learned she wasn't a Christian but she did believe that the Bible was God's word. With that established, Matt started into the study.

He was a lot slower than Robert. He did his best to follow the outline, but he mixed up two Scriptures at one point and then dropped his Bible on the ground when he tried to correct his error. He knew his face was red and he waited for Robert to just take over the study since he was botching it so badly.

But Robert didn't. He corrected Matt on the verses he'd mixed up and injected a comment here and there, but for the most part he let Matt run the show. If he was amused at Matt's fumbling he hid it quite well.

Finally, Matt got to the end of the study. He took a deep breath, and asked, "Would you like to become a Christian?"

The woman dropped her head. "No," she said.

Matt's heart sank. "Why not?" he blurted out.

The woman glanced up at him. "I am at home."

Matt frowned. The statement made no sense to him. Robert leaned forward. "You know what God has to say about that."

"I know, I know," the woman said. "But right now that is what I am. I cannot change."

Matt was confused. "I don't understand," he said.

The woman repeated, "I am at home."

Robert sighed. "She means that a man she's not married to is supporting her right now. That's what 'at home' means here."

"Oh!" Matt said. "But could you get married?"

She shook her head. "He does not want to get married. Right now I cannot become a Christian. Maybe later."

"God doesn't promise us tomorrow," Robert pointed out.

"Yes, yes, I know," the woman agreed. "But I cannot now."

Matt gave Robert a questioning look. Robert shrugged. "Is there nothing we can say to change your mind?" Robert asked.

"No, no," Melinda said. "I cannot become a Christian now."

"Okay," Robert said. "Matt, go ahead and sign her paper. Melinda, know the church is here for you if you change your mind."

Matt signed her paper, feeling bummed out. One of the women who was helping out – Matt recognized her as Barry's mom – came over at Robert's wave and escorted Melinda inside.

Matt stared at the study book. "What'd I do wrong?"

"Nothing," Robert said. "I mean, you mixed a couple of verses up but that's not why she said no."

"But what else should I have said?"

"There was nothing else to say," Robert replied. "Trust me, Matt, you did fine. Some people just don't want to hear the message."

Matt handed the notebook back to Robert. "I think you should do the next one."

"Okay," Robert said. "But you did your job, Matt. You were the watchman. Don't let this get you down."

That was easy to say. But, as Matt watched Robert stand to greet a squat dark-skinned woman, he knew it wasn't easy to do.

- NINETEEN -

O KAY, THAT'S IT FOR TODAY," Robert said, glancing at his watch.
"What? Already?" Matt said, surprised.

Robert grinned. "It's 4:30, man. We gotta let the docs finish up with the people we've sent them."

Matt couldn't believe how quickly the time had gone. "This was really interesting."

"I know," Robert said. "I bet if you study some over the weekend you'll do even better with it."

Matt grimaced. "I didn't do so well the first time out."

Robert shook his head. "Don't you get it?" He waved his hand to where others were wrapping up individual Bible studies. "Most people say no. It wasn't you."

"But how can people say they understand it and still say no?" Matt asked as he pulled out his water bottle and drained it.

"C'mon," Robert said. As they walked into the church building he continued, "It's like the Bible says. The road's narrow, and only a few find it."

Matt pulled aside the sheet that served as a door to the break room and let Robert duck inside. "But that's discouraging. I hate hearing one 'no' – I don't know how I'd handle hearing it again and again."

Two older women and Jenna's dad were sitting in the break room. Robert greeted everyone while Matt refilled his water bottle.

Matt noted how easy it was for Robert to talk to the adults. He knew everyone's name and even knew one of the women had just become a grandmother. Matt hadn't remembered that at all.

The room was crowded with five people, so Matt and Robert left after Robert refilled his water bottle. Once outside the room, Matt asked, "How do you keep from being discouraged?"

"I told you," Robert said, "I realize I'm just the messenger. It's not me they're rejecting – it's God."

Matt frowned. "That sounds a lot simpler than it feels."

"I know," Robert said. "I remember the first time I started doing studies last year. I got really bummed out with all the negative answers. Brother Harry's the one who showed me the passage in Ezekiel. That helped a lot."

Matt sighed. "There's just so many . . . "

"Hey, you never know, that gal might change her mind. Sometimes it just takes people a while to think things through."

"I hope she does," Matt said. There'd been five baptisms that day, including the young lady Robert had studied with. The excitement surrounding them had been infectious, though it hadn't completely pierced his depression over Melinda.

Soon the last of the patients were dismissed and it was time to set up for the gospel meeting. As Matt helped move benches into place, he scanned the people milling about, looking for Melinda.

He didn't see her. But he felt a tug at his pants leg. Looking down, he saw Barry staring up at him. The boy quickly gave Matt an exaggerated pout, his eyes twinkling.

"Oh, ho," Matt said, crouching down. "So that's how it's gonna be?"

Barry nodded, still holding the pout.

"Okay, what did I say the other day? No smiling, now . . . "

It wasn't long before Barry was giggling, his small hands in front of his mouth trying to keep them in. Matt couldn't help but grin back.

"Looks like you made a friend," Jenna said, coming up to stand beside them.

Matt stood up quickly. "Yeah, I guess. Um . . . how'd it go with the kids?"

"Fine," Jenna said. "How'd it go with the Bible studies?"

"I . . . " Matt stammered. "Well, there were five baptisms."

"That's great!" Jenna said. She looked over Matt's shoulder. "Oh, there's someone I want to talk to before we get started. Excuse me."

She left, and Matt felt like a dork. Why couldn't he talk to her?

Another tug at his pants leg brought his attention back to Barry. He was trying to pout again.

Matt shook his head. "I can do this as long as you can," he told the little boy, crouching down again.

* * *

"So, how did today go?" Anil asked when Matt slid into the front seat.

"It went okay," Matt said. "The studies were very interesting."

"That sounds good," said Anil. "Just a moment." He stepped out of the van to talk to another driver while members of the team climbed in.

People moved more slowly than they had at the beginning of the week. Matt noticed his mother rested her head on the back of the seat with her eyes closed. Everyone was tired and looking forward to a day off tomorrow.

Anil slammed the doors shut and got into the van. "Okay, here we go," he said to Matt as they pulled out. "So you just sat and listened today? I am surprised you were not bored."

"Well, I got to do a study," Matt said.

"And how did that go?" Anil asked.

Matt grimaced. "She said no. She's 'at home' or something like that."

"Ah, yes, that is very difficult," Anil said with a nod. "It is part of our culture, yes? Very hard to fight against."

"Yeah," Matt said, feeling gloomy. He stared out the front window, for once not reacting to Anil's driving.

Anil gave him a sharp look. "You think you were at fault?"

"I guess," Matt said.

"Did you do your best? Did you give her the gospel message?"

"Yeah. I mean, Robert helped me some, but yeah, we gave her the message."

"Then what else could you do?" Anil asked. "You could not force her into the water. It is her choice. You did what you were supposed to do."

"That's what Robert said," Matt sighed.

"Robert is correct." Anil paused as he leaned on his horn and swerved around a slower moving vehicle. Once they were back in their proper lane he continued. "In fact, it sounds like you are taking my advice. So tell me, how do you feel about Guyana today?"

Matt thought about it for a minute. "I dunno. I got real excited about things when people were getting baptized, you know? But other than that – I don't know how I feel."

Anil grinned. "That is an improvement. Tomorrow I will show you something special and perhaps you will think even better of my country."

Matt scratched at one of the numerous bug bites on his arm. He'd let one of the nurses spray him with repellent, but it didn't seem to deter the mosquitoes from snacking on him.

He realized he hadn't thought about being uncomfortable most of the day. He'd been too caught up in the Bible studies, in the people, to remember that he was hot and bug-bitten.

Was it possible he'd found the answer to his bad attitude? Matt wasn't sure. All he knew was that even though he was hot, tired, and hungry at the moment he wasn't feeling nearly as depressed as he had been all week. Even being bummed out about his first Bible study, he still felt somewhat upbeat thanks to the baptisms.

Was God finally answering his prayer?

* * *

After the devotional, Steve Lockwood called Matt over to him. Wondering what he'd done now, Matt dragged himself over to where the bearded man was standing with Stan

"Stan tells me you did all right today," Lockwood said.

"Robert told me how things had gone," Stan said. "And I was keeping an eye on you – you even did a study yourself, I see."

"It didn't go very well," Matt said.

Lockwood shook his head. "That's not what I heard. Stan says you did pretty good for your first try."

"But she said no," Matt pointed out. "How's that good?"

Stan snorted. "If we judged how good our Bible studies went by the response of the student we'd all be doing badly, Matt. People say 'no' a lot more often than they say 'yes.'"

"Stan is right," Lockwood confirmed. "The fact you tried – well, it seems you're trying to make up for the beginning of the week. I'm glad to see it."

Matt said nothing. He knew his attitude still needed work but he was afraid to say anything about it.

"Let's hope the next week is better," Lockwood said. "Have fun tomorrow. Anil says you're going to Kaieteur National Park with him? You'll love it."

"Yes sir," Matt said.

"See you at breakfast tomorrow," Stan told him.

Taking Stan's statement as a dismissal, Matt said good night and left the two men. He headed to his room, thinking about the next day with mixed feelings.

What did Anil want to show him? And how would it change his view of Guyana?

- TWENTY -

WHEN THE ALARM on Matt's phone went off the next morning, he groaned and slapped at it. The phone tumbled off the nightstand and landed on the floor, still buzzing.

Muttering threats against the device under his breath, Matt got out of bed long enough to turn the alarm off and place it back on the nightstand. He then flopped back onto his cot and buried his head into his pillow.

"Hey Matt?" Robert asked sleepily from the next cot, "Aren't you getting up?"

"Shut up," Matt mumbled into the pillow. He'd stayed up late the night before playing cards with Brad and Chuck. Suddenly sleeping in seemed like a lot better plan than going off to some national park.

Robert yawned. "What about the trip?" Robert was a part of the group that was going to the park that day.

"You go on the trip. You can tell me about it when you get back, okay?"

"That what you want me to tell your folks?" Robert asked as he swung his legs out of bed.

Matt groaned again. "I'm not getting up yet."

"Okay," Robert said. "I'll get the bathroom first then."

"Knock yourself out."

When the bathroom door shut. Matt firmly shut his eyes but he found he couldn't go back to sleep. Righteous Robert was right. Sleeping in wasn't worth the hassle he'd have with his folks if he bailed on the trip. After all, it had been his idea.

He wondered what he'd been thinking. Anil had made it sound grand, like some big adventure. At the moment all Matt could think of was tromping around some rainforest under a hot sun. At the moment, that didn't sound very appealing.

But Jenna would be going on the trip as well. Matt thought about her and his stomach did a little flip-flop. He still liked her a lot, but he wondered what she thought of him. He still remembered her "jerk" comment from earlier in the week. Had she changed her mind?

Robert came out of the bathroom moments later, humming some tune under his breath. Matt thought it sounded like one of the songs they'd sung at the devotional the night before. For some reason it got his back up.

"Bathroom's all yours," Robert announced.

"Thanks, Rig – Robert," Matt said, reluctantly swinging his legs out of bed. He bit his lip. That had been close.

He dragged himself to the bathroom and got ready to start the day.

* * *

"My, that plane looks . . . small," Matt's mom said as they piled out of the black-and-white van that had picked them up at the hotel.

Matt glanced at it. The plane was a prop jet, its propellers still in the sultry morning air. His interest stirred slightly. He'd never ridden in a plane that small before.

Anil grinned. "Don't worry, ma'am, the plane is perfectly safe. It will be a good flight and a good day!"

Matt rolled his eyes. He was still tired and Anil's cheerfulness was starting to get on his nerves.

They entered the small hangar and everyone began checking in at the counter that stood at one end of the room. A few chairs were scattered about and Matt dropped into one, figuring his dad would get him checked in just fine.

He was pulling out his earbuds when Anil sat next to him. The Guyanese man looked unhappy. "What is wrong?"

"Nothing," Matt said. He stifled a yawn. "I'm just tired, okay?"

"You act like you are here against your will," Anil argued. "You agreed to come."

"I'm here and I'm not complaining," Matt griped. "That should be good enough."

Anil's mouth formed a thin line. "This is a trip that is not cheap. You should want to get something out of it."

"If it's so expensive, how can you be going?" Matt asked

He regretted the question the moment it left his mouth. Anil stared at him with a hurt expression. He then got up without another word and went to the check-in counter.

Matt groaned. What was wrong with him? It wasn't any of his business how Anil could afford the trip. And Anil was right – it had been Matt's idea. Maybe a bad decision on his part, but still his decision.

He bit his lip as he stared at Anil's stiff back, wondering if he'd just lost a friend.

* * *

Matt didn't get a chance to talk to Anil before it was time to get on the prop jet. The Guyanese man made it a point to stay away from Matt and speak to others in the group.

Matt tried to hang back when it was time to board, hoping to catch Anil before he got on the plane, but his parents insisted he get in line with them. Matt slumped into a window seat while his parents took two seats across from him.

Anil was among the last to board. He was chatting with Robert and he glanced at the remaining seats. The one next to Matt was empty, and he tried to offer it to Anil.

For a moment Anil hesitated. Then with a resigned sigh, he sat down next to Matt. Robert went past them to take a seat behind them.

Matt found it impossible to look at Anil once he'd sat next to him. He concentrated on the co-pilot, who gave the typical safety instructions for a plane. Once he finished, he went back to the cockpit. Moments later the plane began to move.

Once the plane was in the air, Matt leaned towards Anil. Under cover of the loud engines, he said in the man's ear, "I'm sorry. I said something stupid again, didn't I?"

"You aren't sure?" Anil asked, turning to face Matt.

Matt sighed. "It was stupid, okay? It's none of my business."

"No, it is not," Anil agreed. "But I will tell you anyway. I have saved up for this trip – I wanted to go once this year. Steve Lockwood also helped me; he said it would be good for me to spend some time with some of the team."

Matt shifted in his seat. He hadn't thought of the cost of the trip when he'd suggested it, and his parents hadn't raised any kind of issues with paying for it.

It was easy to forget that money wasn't a problem for his family. Matt simply took it for granted that they had enough for their needs and then some.

"I guess I'm pretty lucky," Matt said.

"No. You are blessed," Anil corrected. "But then again, I am as well. God has chosen to bless us in different ways."

Matt was stunned. How could Anil still think he was blessed? He wanted to ask him that but was afraid it would come out as another stupid question.

Anil must have seen the question in his eyes, because a small smile touched his lips. "Yes, I am blessed. I am healthy. I have work. My family has shelter and enough to eat." He shrugged. "These are gifts from God – I know others who do not have these good things."

Matt thought about it. Had he ever considered good health a blessing? It was something else he'd taken for granted – aside from a bout of chicken pox when he was eight, he couldn't recall any serious illnesses.

"I never thought of those things as blessings," Matt admitted.

"Perhaps that is why you are having problems with your attitude," Anil said. "Because you are not thankful."

"Ow," Matt said. "That was blunt."

Anil was unapologetic. "That is how my people are. I have heard Steve talk to Americans about us – your people tend to, how do you say it, not say what you think outright? There is a saying, something to do with a bush?"

Matt thought about it. "You mean beat around the bush?"

"Yes!" Anil said. "You beat around the bush. My people, we do not do this. We speak plainly. We also want people to speak with us in this manner."

The plane bounced slightly as it encountered some turbulence, making Matt grab his armrest. When the ride smoothed out, he took a gulp of his bottled water. "So you think I'm ungrateful?"

"You admit you haven't given thought to your blessings," Anil pointed out. "How can you thank God for things you are not aware of?"

"I guess you have a point," Matt said. He hoped no one could hear this conversation. He listened and realized the noise from the engines was masking the other chats going on in the plane so his was probably not being heard by anyone else, especially his parents.

"You should learn to count your blessings," Anil said. "The Bible says to give thanks for everything and in every circumstance. Paul was thankful even chained to a soldier in prison. You are not in prison."

"That's true," Matt said. "But I didn't want to come to Guyana, remember? I didn't exactly want to be here."

"So this is a good place to practice," Anil said. "If you can be thankful in Guyana, surely you can be thankful when you return to America."

Matt glanced out the window. He saw they were in a mountainous region, green trees dotting the slopes. He hadn't realized there were mountains in Guyana.

"So you're saying if I'm thankful my attitude will magically change?" Matt asked, turning back to face Anil.

"No, no magic," Anil said. "And it will take time. You have let your bad attitude stay with you a while."

"I've been trying," Matt argued.

"I know," Anil said. "And that is good. But did you believe Satan would give up on you so easily? No, he will continue to try to get past your defenses. You must keep on working, not relax your guard."

Matt slumped back in his seat. "That sounds like hard work."

"Of course it is hard work," Anil said. "Living according to the world – it is very easy, yes? That is why so many do so. But to live the right way – that takes effort. But you are not a lazy young man, Matt. I do not believe hard work will stop you."

A comfortable silence settled between the two of them. Matt put in his earbuds and turned on his music. He closed his eyes and thought about things he could be thankful for.

He must have dozed off, because the next thing he knew Anil was shaking his shoulder. "Look. Look, Matt!"

Matt opened his eyes and looked out the window. He stared.

The waterfall was huge. Matt had never seen one so tall. A rainbow arced above the cloud of spray that obscured the bottom of the falls.

Anil looked over his shoulder. "Kaieteur Falls. That is where we are going."

- TWENTY-ONE -

A FTER CIRCLING THE FALLS, the plane landed at a nearby landing strip. Everyone spilled out of the plane, including the copilot, who would also serve as their guide. He introduced himself as George and hauled out a cooler filled with bottled water. "You should take," he urged them. "Drink lots of water here in the jungle."

Matt took a deep breath. The jungle. He was definitely not in America. The sun beat down and he quickly drained his bottle before refilling the plastic container with one of the bottles from the cooler.

There was a small wooden building near the strip. A small wooden sign next to it read, "Welcome to Kaieteur National Park." George told them that there were restrooms in the building if anyone needed them. "Then we will begin our walk."

Matt caught floral scents in the air. He didn't know much about flowers so he couldn't tell what he was smelling. Maybe his mom could tell, she was looking around with a huge smile on her face. Others were already snapping pictures of the plane and the welcome building.

Matt took a few steps away from the group. He wondered what Anil expected him to find here. It was a park. Nothing special . .

. well, that waterfall had looked impressive. Anil said they were heading there.

"Oh, look," Matt's mom said, pointing to Matt's right pants leg. He looked down and saw a small grasshopper on his dark blue slacks. It was sandy colored with a bit of green and orange near its head.

At once everyone was taking a picture of the insect. Matt froze, feeling a little embarrassed at all the attention, even if it wasn't on him specifically.

Anil grinned at him. "You want me to take a picture for you?" he asked, holding up a small camera.

Matt shook his head. "That's okay." He looked down at the critter and shrugged. "I don't know what the big deal is."

"It's easier to see on your pants leg then on the ground," Robert said, snapping a shot of his own with his phone's camera. "That's the attraction."

George seemed to enjoy the situation. "Yes, we will see many wonderful things on our walk. As soon as everyone is ready, we will go."

Once those who'd opted for a bathroom break rejoined the group, they started walking on a trail. Matt managed to let his parents get ahead of him on the narrow path and found himself with Robert and Anil. Jenna and her parents brought up the rear.

The guide began to describe the foliage around them. Matt tuned most of it out. It was humid among the trees and he caught the word, "rainforest."

Anil asked, "Do you have anything like this in America?"

"No way," Robert said. "This is amazing."

"It's a forest," Matt said. "Just wetter than ours."

Robert frowned. "It's way different from any forests we have. It's not as . . .civilized, for one thing."

Matt couldn't argue with that. The trail appeared to be barely maintained. It was narrow enough that plants brushed his arms as he went by.

He could hear frogs croaking off the path, along with the chirp of birds. He heard Jenna's mother behind him wondering about poisonous snakes.

The guide stopped them here and urged them to be quiet. "Look over there," he said, pointing into the foliage. "A cock-of-the-rock. Very special."

Matt spotted the pigeon sized bird, it's orange plumage bright against the green plants around it. He used his phone's camera to zoom in for a better look.

"Cock-of-the-rock is very rare. Does not do well in captivity," the guide continued. "Its feathers are valued for decoration, but it is illegal to capture it – you could go to jail for fifty years if you caught one."

Matt was surprised. He snapped a picture of the bird. It didn't look that special to him, but someone obviously thought it was.

The group continued through the rainforest. They crossed a couple of brooks, and Matt was getting bored. The rainforest seemed to go on forever.

They heard the falls before they saw them. It started as a distant roar that grew louder as the trees and foliage began to thin. They came to a lookout point some distance from the falls, and Matt got his second look at them.

"Kaieteur Falls," George said. "It is one of the world's highest single-drop waterfalls. Europeans discovered the falls in 1870."

Matt stared at the falls while the guide droned on. He stepped a little closer to the edge of the lookout to get a better view.

"Matt . . . " his mother's worried voice sounded behind him.

"It's okay, Emily," his dad assured her.

Something about the falls stirred something in Matt. Even from this distance he could get a sense of their power. He brought his phone up and snapped a quick picture.

"We will get closer," the guide promised. "When you all are ready, we will continue."

Closer? Matt felt a grin tug at his lips. Yes, closer would be good.

The group walked down the trail The guide continued to spout statistics about the falls as they traveled. The sound of the falls grew louder and Matt felt the sound enter his bones.

Finally, they stopped. The guide pointed out some small signs that read, "Please keep 8 feet away from the edge of the cliff."

"Be careful here," he said. I do not want to lose a tourist today."

Matt barely heard him. He was entranced.

They were close to the top of the falls – close enough to feel spray on his face from the cascading water. Foamy brown water poured the edge to fall far, far below.

Matt stepped to the edge and knelt. The falls landed in a shining, twisting ribbon of water. He could see a rainbow in the spray.

"Matt? That's too close," his father called. "Come on back, son."

Matt wanted to keep looking but he could hear the nervousness in his father's voice. He carefully got to his feet and stepped back from the edge.

Anil came to stand next to him. "Impressive, is it not?"

"Yeah," Matt agreed. "It's huge."

"741 feet down," George told him. "You stay away from edge, that is a long drop."

Matt nodded. He turned back to see the rest of the group taking pictures of the falls from a safe distance. Jenna was looking at him with wide eyes. He noticed she stood quite a ways from the edge.

Anil put an arm around Matt's shoulders. "Dr. Brooks? Please take a picture of us together?"

Matt's father held up his phone. "All right you two, smile."

Matt grinned. As soon as the photo was shot he turned again and began to take pictures of the falls.

"This is what I wanted to show you," Anil said to Matt. He gazed at the falls as he spoke, his voice raised to combat the sound of the falling water. "Do you see?"

"I do see it," Matt said. "It's impressive."

"If you had never come to Guyana, you would never have seen this evidence of God's handiwork," Anil continued. "And you would have been poorer for it."

Matt turned and looked at Anil. "I guess that's true."

"It is true," Anil insisted. "You came here not willing to give Guyana or this trip a chance. You only came to endure. But see what you would have missed!"

Matt struggled to understand what the Guyanese man was saying. Was he right? "But I'm trying to do better."

"And you still struggle," Anil said. "You must devote yourself to change, not just try. Then you will find more gifts besides the Kaieteur Falls."

Matt turned back to the falls. He knew the verse Romans 1:20: " For the invisible things of him from the creation of the world are clearly seen, being understood by the things that are made, even his eternal power and Godhead; so that they are without excuse…"

Looking at the Kaietuer Falls, Matt felt that he understood the verse better than he ever had before.

* * *

After the group hiked back to the airstrip, they were flown to a nearby resort where a buffet lunch was laid out outside.

Suddenly Matt was starving. He stood impatiently in line behind Jenna and her parents. They were filled with talk about the park but Matt was content to just listen. Anil stood with him, and seemed willing to be quiet for a change.

Matt loaded his plate with baked chicken, rice, and carrots. He sat with his folks at one of the picnic tables. Robert and Anil joined them, and conversation flowed around Matt.

He thought about what Anil had said at the falls. If he were being honest, he hadn't really been giving the trip a chance. He'd simply been looking for ways to get through it with the least amount of pain.

Maybe that was the wrong approach. Maybe instead of trying to endure his remaining time here, he should try to embrace it? Could he do that? Was it even possible?

And what would happen if he did?

- TWENTY-TWO -

MATT WOKE UP SUNDAY MORNING with no clear decision made. That annoyed him.

How hard could this be? He asked himself as he showered. *Keep up what I'm doing. Or turn into Righteous Robert? Ugh, I don't want to do that!*

Matt hadn't wanted to come to Guyana. That hadn't changed. But he was warming to the country. Should he take the next step, and act like this was a great idea? Admit maybe that his parents were right?

Matt felt his pride rear up at that thought. How could he admit that? Wouldn't he be having a better time if he'd been allowed to stay home? He'd certainly be more comfortable physically.

He wrestled with those thoughts as he went down to breakfast. To his surprise, he saw that Jenna wasn't there with her folks. Neither was his mom in the dining room, though his dad was there talking to Stan.

Matt and Robert walked up to the two men. Dr. Brooks was talking. " – encourage everyone to wash their hands frequently. We'll see if we can keep this contained."

Stan nodded. "I'll make an announcement. I hope Emily feels better soon."

"Is Mom all right?" Matt asked.

"Your mom has some kind of stomach bug," his dad replied. "So does Jenna Trask and Dr. Lopez and his wife. She'll be fine, she's just pretty miserable at the moment."

"Oh," Matt said. That was a bummer, being sick. Especially being sick in a foreign country.

"You boys need to be sure and wash your hands before eating," Matt's dad continued. "Use the hand sanitizers we brought. We're going to try to keep this from running through the team, if possible."

Both boys nodded. "Anything else we can do, sir?" Robert asked.

"Thank you Robert, but I can't think of anything," Matt's dad said. "We should get some breakfast before we head to worship. Come on."

Matt got in line for the buffet, his mind drifting back to his earlier thoughts. What should he do?

* * *

Because the clinic was still set up in the auditorium, the worship service was set up in the unfinished room next door. Matt took a seat near the back with his father.

Anil was there, dressed in a crisp tan dress shirt and tie. He waved at Matt and sat in front, next to Harry.

Matt tried to focus on the service, but his mind kept wandering. He was a little worried about his mom. Dad said it wasn't serious, but what if it was? What if she had to go to the hospital?

He was brought out of his thoughts when Harry stood up and introduced Anil as the speaker that morning. Matt sat up a little straighter, wondering what his friend would have to say.

Anil smiled at the congregation. He stood in front of them with his Bible open in his hand. "I want to thank you for the opportunity to speak to you from God's word. Today I will be reading from Philippians, chapter two, verses five through eleven. It reads:

'Let this mind be in you, which was also in Christ Jesus: Who, being in the form of God, thought it not robbery to be equal with God: But made himself of no reputation, and took upon him the form of a servant, and was made in the likeness of men: And being found in fashion as a man, he humbled himself, and became obedient unto death, even the death of the cross.

"Wherefore God also hath highly exalted him, and given him a name which is above every name: That at the name of Jesus every knee should bow, of things in heaven, and things in earth, and things under the earth; And that every tongue should confess that Jesus Christ is Lord, to the glory of God the Father.'"

Anil closed his Bible. "We are supposed to have the same attitude as Jesus. He didn't think about Himself while he was on the earth. He put us first and Himself last, even to the point of dying on the cross for us."

Matt used his phone to access the verse Anil had read. He found himself feeling annoyed – it was almost as if Anil had picked this topic specifically to target him.

While Anil continued to speak, Matt studied the verses. Jesus had been forced to deal with a lot more than heat and insects. Matt had seen the movie "The Passion." He'd found the depictions of the torture Jesus endured disturbing.

Jesus was the prime example of a good attitude. Matt chewed his lip. He knew his own attitude wasn't at all Christlike. But how did he change it?

He tuned back in to what Anil was saying. "And how do we gain this attitude? Romans twelve, verse two says 'And be not conformed to this world: but be ye transformed by the renewing of your mind, that ye may prove what is that good, and acceptable, and perfect, will of God.' We need to change how we think."

That's great, Matt thought. But how?

As if he'd asked the question out loud, Anil continued. "How, you may ask, do we renew our minds? We put something different into it. We find this different stuff by studying God's word every day and praying to Him for guidance and wisdom. Then we will see the changes we want."

Matt felt disappointed. Bible study and prayer? That seemed to be a preacher's answer to everything. Matt wanted something more . . . something he could do that would flip a switch in his brain so he'd have the right kind of attitude.

Anil finished up his sermon. "There may be someone here who is ready to become a Christian. Or, perhaps you are a child of God but you have struggles right now. Whatever your needs are, come forward and let us know of them as we stand and sing."

Matt stood with his father and began to sing "Just As I Am." He mouthed the well-known words but his mind was far away from them.

He was certainly struggling. But did he want to go forward? Tell everyone there what was going on and ask them to pray for him? He felt a stab of trepidation at the thought.

Part of him was tempted though. He knew he was having a hard time with it on his own . . . maybe others could help him, give him better advice.

He argued with himself throughout the song and then it was over and too late to act. Matt sat back down with the rest of the congregation, feeling confused and dissatisfied.

- TWENTY-THREE -

As the members of the team got back into the van, Matt confronted Anil. He had to wait until several people had paused to compliment the young man on his sermon. By the time Matt got to him, Anil had a broad grin on his face. "Ready to go, Matt?"

Matt glared at him. "Did you aim that sermon at me?" he demanded.

Anil's smile slipped. He sighed. "You were on my heart when I wrote the sermon. We have talked so much about what you are going through, it seemed to me an appropriate topic."

Matt scowled. "So you think if I just study enough and pray enough my attitude will change?"

"You are not the only one in the world to have to deal with a bad attitude," Anil said. "And there is much to talk about on this subject – more than a sermon could cover. Come, get in the van, we can talk."

Matt was tempted to find a seat in another van, but he could see they were filling up behind him. Going to another vehicle seemed almost like running away, too.

He climbed into the front seat as more people came to speak with Anil. He stuck his earbuds into his ears and turned on his iPod, staring out of the streaked windshield.

When Anil climbed into the driver's seat, Matt didn't look at him or speak to him. His silence continued for the entire drive back to the hotel.

* * *

"Hey Matt," Robert said as Matt was finishing lunch, "I was going to see how Jenna's feeling. Want to come? We can say hi to your mom first if you want."

"Sure," Matt said. He'd been thinking of a nap, then a dip in the pool, but Robert had reminded him that his mother was sick. He felt a stab of guilt at that thought.

After he wiped his mouth and drained his water glass he and Robert headed to his parents' room. To his relief his mom didn't look that bad. She was pale and a little shaky but she was dressed, sitting up at the desk and surfing the Internet.

"I'll be fine," she assured Matt. "Your dad thinks this is a 24-hour bug. "I'm just resting and drinking a lot of fluids."

"Can I get you anything?" Matt asked. He felt funny – usually it was his mom asking this of him, not the other way around.

"No, your dad brought me more water," his mother said. "It's just a stomach bug, sweetheart. Don't worry."

Matt felt a little better leaving his parents' room. He and Robert headed to Jenna's room, one floor up.

When Mrs. Trask let them in, Matt saw Jenna lying in bed. She gave them a weak smile. "Hi."

Matt and Robert sat down on the opposite twin bed. Matt noticed the room was a little bigger than his and Robert's. "Hey, you got a real bed," he joked. "Robert and I have cots to deal with."

Robert said, "I guess we got a cheap room."

Jenna's mom said, "They are renovating the hotel. They've upgraded the rooms on this floor, I'm told, and are doing the rest when they get the chance." She handed Jenna a bottle of water. "Honey, you know what Dr. Brooks said – you have to drink more water if you want to feel better."

Jenna made a face but obediently took a drink of water. Matt thought she looked worse than his mom and started to worry again.

The two boys didn't stay long. After a few minutes of small talk, they excused themselves and headed back to their room.

Matt pulled out his swim trunks and went into the bathroom to change. When he came out, Robert was stretched out on his cot, his eyes shut. "You okay there?" Matt asked, wondering if Robert was coming down with what the others had.

"Yeah, just gonna catch a nap here," Robert said without opening his eyes.

"Okay," Matt said and headed down to the pool.

He saw he wasn't the only one with the idea. Brad and Chuck were already in the water, laughing and splashing water on each other. A few other members of the team were swimming or sitting in one of the white plastic chairs that were scattered around the perimeter of the pool.

Matt dropped his towel on one of the empty chairs and climbed into the pool. The cool water was a shock at first until he eased his body into the deeper part of the pool.

Swimming helped Matt clear his mind a bit. He prayed while he swam, for the sick members of the team, especially his mother and Jenna. He prayed about his attitude, asking God to show him how to change it.

Once again, he was disappointed to find his feelings hadn't changed. He got out of the pool and grabbed his towel, wondering what he should do. He needed answers and it felt as if God wasn't providing them.

When he got back to the room, Robert was still asleep. Matt moved around quietly, grabbing a quick shower and throwing on a pair of shorts and a t-shirt. At the hotel the dress code was relaxed a bit, much to Matt's relief.

He picked up his cell phone and turned back to Philippians chapter two. Have the same mind as Jesus . . . but how? No one seemed to have a clear answer for him. Anil had mentioned deciding to change – but hadn't Matt already done that?

He groaned and flopped back on his cot. All he was getting out of this was a headache.

"You okay?"

Matt turned his head. Robert's eyes were open and he was looking at Matt with a look of concern.

"Sorry. Didn't mean to wake you," Matt said.

"Nah, I was already waking up," Robert said. He stretched and swung his legs off the cot. "What's wrong?"

Matt was about to brush him off when he thought about it. Robert seemed to have his act together – maybe he had some insight in this.

"You listen to the sermon today?" Matt asked, sitting up in turn.

"Yeah," Robert said.

"Okay, here's the thing. Anil talked about changing your mind, to be more like Jesus, right?"

"Right."

"Okay, but how do you do that? Anil mentioned prayer and Bible study, but everyone always say that for any problem."

"Because it's usually the answer," Robert said. "But you're not satisfied with that?"

Matt blew out a huff of frustration. "I've been praying, okay? I keep asking God to change my attitude, but it isn't changing."

"You're trying to change your attitude?"

Matt mentally rolled his eyes. He'd let slip more of what was going on in his head then he'd meant to. But he was committed now, he supposed. "Look, I know my attitude has been bad, okay? I know I need to change it. I just can't figure out how."

Robert's face grew thoughtful. "Well, there's something that might help, but I don't know what you'll think of it."

"What?"

Robert grabbed his Bible from the floor by his cot. He flipped some pages and then stopped. "First Thessalonians, chapter five, verses sixteen through eighteen. 'Rejoice evermore. Pray without ceasing. In every thing give thanks: for this is the will of God in Christ Jesus concerning you.'"

Matt frowned. "I don't get it. I told you I'd been praying."

"Okay, but how have you been praying?" Robert asked. "This passage talks about rejoicing and giving thanks. Are you being thankful?"

"About being here in Guyana?" Matt asked. "Robert, I never wanted to be here in the first place."

"Okay, so you aren't thankful for Guyana. What *are* you thankful for?" Robert asked.

Matt had to stop and think. What was he thankful for? "Well . . . " he said, "I'm thankful that Mom is gonna be okay."

"That's a start," Robert said. "How about your blessings?"

"My blessings?" Matt asked. "What, like thanking God for Jesus' dying on the cross and stuff like that?"

"Partly," said Robert. "But what about things like your health? The material things you have? Coming to Guyana, I always realize how much I really have compared to others."

"My health?" Matt said. "That's a blessing?"

Robert shrugged. "You should know, being a doctor's son, not everyone has that. So yeah, it's a blessing."

Matt wasn't sure he agreed. It must have shown on his face, because Robert frowned. He leaned over and grabbed his backpack from the end of the bed and dug through it until he found a notebook. Robert tore a blank page out of it and handed it to Matt.

"Here," he said. "List ten things you can be thankful for. Then pray to God and thank Him for each one."

Matt took the paper. "You're giving me homework?"

"Hey, you asked me for advice," Robert retorted. He got up from his cot. "I'm going for a walk. You let me know how it goes."

When Robert left the room, Matt went to the desk with the piece of paper. He found a pen on the desk and held it over the blank page, trying to think of something to be thankful for.

Moments passed. He began to doodle on a corner of the page. What a stupid idea. What did he have to be thankful for?

What about what God has given you?

Matt considered that thought, tapping his pen on the paper. Okay, fair enough. What had God given him?

Slowly, with long pauses in between, Matt began to write.

- TWENTY-FOUR -

MATT DIDN'T MENTION his list to Robert when the teen returned to the room. In fact, they didn't speak much at all the rest of the afternoon before dinner. Matt was wrestling with the things Robert had said and didn't feel up to another conversation with the teen.

His mother wasn't at dinner. Neither was Jenna. Dr. and Mrs. Lopez made an appearance, both looking tired but otherwise all right. They didn't eat any dinner, content to drink some hot tea instead.

Matt's dad assured him that his mother felt much better and would be at the devotional later that evening. Matt was glad to hear that and guessed that could be another item on his "thankful list."

Stan came by Matt's table where he, his father, and Robert sat eating. He said to Robert, "We're going to have a time of prayer tonight for our devotional. Think you could lead one?"

"Sure," Robert said. "Any particular topic?"
"We'll discuss that tonight," Stan said. "I'm going to be asking for requests. Certainly it'll be about the week to come."

"Okay, no problem," Robert said.

"Great," Stan said. "David, how's Emily feeling?"

"Better," Matt's dad said. "She'll be at the devotional tonight."

"Great. See you all in a few," Stan said as he moved on to another table.

Matt took a bite of rice. He felt a little jealous that Stan had no problem asking Robert to pray, but not him. It wasn't like Matt hadn't led a prayer before – he did sometimes back home.

Then he felt badly. Given how his attitude had been, why was he surprised? He wasn't exactly being the shining example of Christ here, was he? Even though he was trying to do better, it was clear he wasn't doing good enough.

Suddenly not hungry anymore, he excused himself from the table. He found himself wandering the hotel's halls, feeling restless.

He found himself back on the roof of the Phoenix, alone for the moment. Matt leaned on the parapet of the roof and pulled his list out of his pocket.

Under the garish light of the hotel's sign behind him, Matt read over his list.

1.   my health
2.   the Bible
3.   my friends
4.   my home
5.   food
6.   my things
7.   the fact I don't live in Guyana

His mom feeling better would be number eight. If he was going to do this the way Robert had instructed, he needed two more.

Matt wondered what else he could add. It had taken him a long time to come up with these. He rubbed his temple, a headache starting to grow.

Well, maybe this would be a good enough start. Matt bowed his head. "God, I want to change my attitude. I know I keep saying this, but nothing seems to be working so far, though I am trying."

He opened his eyes and gazed at his list. "I made this list of things I'm thankful for. I know there should be more – help me find them. But in the meantime, thank you for these. Help me appreciate my blessings more. In Jesus' name, amen."

He heard the door behind him open and he quickly folded up his list, jamming it back into his back pocket. He saw Stan step onto the roof, a Bible in his hand.

"Oh, hi there, Matt," Stan said. "You're here early."

"Uh, yeah," Matt said. He felt embarrassed, as if he'd been caught doing something wrong. "I found out this is a good place to think."

Stan nodded. "I can see why it would be." The older man came to stand next to Matt, leaning on the parapet. "Penny for your thoughts."

Matt squirmed. "Well…"

"None of my business?" Stan asked with a grin.

Matt felt his face grow hot. "It's just that I'm really trying to figure out some things."

"Anything I can do to help?"

Matt thought about how the past week had gone. He thought about how this was the third person this week – after Anil and Robert – who offered to help him.

But this was Stan Conner, head of the team. Opening up to Anil had been one thing – the Guyanese man had been persistent. Talking to Robert had been impulsive. Somehow bringing this up to Stan wasn't something Matt was ready to do.

He sighed. "I guess you could pray for me."

"I can do that," Stan agreed. "Anything in particular?"

Matt suddenly found the lights of Georgetown fascinating. He swallowed. "I guess . . . that this week goes better than the last one?"

"Sounds good," Stan said. "I'll definitely pray for you about that."

"Thanks," Matt said. He heard the door to the roof open up again and voices. He didn't turn around until Stan moved away to greet the new arrivals.

Matt moved to one of the chairs located in the rear and sat down. He heard conversations flow around him but didn't take part in any of them. He was too busy thinking.

Finally everyone was seated. Stan stood up in front of the team. "So far we've had a great week here in Guyana. We've treated almost a thousand patients and had twelve baptisms. God is truly answering prayers."

"Amen," several people called out.

"Tonight we're going to devote ourselves to prayer, so that the upcoming week will continue to be successful, that we'll continue to meet needs, both physical and spiritual. I've invited some people to come up and lead us in prayer. We'll also take requests, if anyone has one."

Several people raised their hands and asked for prayers. The Trasks asked for Jenna to feel better plus anyone else who was sick. Brad asked for more open hearts in the coming week. Others made requests for people back home in the States.

Stan was wrapping things up when Matt stood up. "Stan? I have a request."

The team leader looked over at him. "Yes, Matt?"

He couldn't believe he was doing this. But quickly, before he lost his nerve and sat back down, he said, "I really would like prayers. I know things didn't go real great for me this week and – and I want to do better." His face burning, he sat down, grateful that no one had decided to sit near him.

"We will all pray for you, Matt," Stan said. "Anyone else?"

No one else spoke up, and the group spent the next few moments in prayer, led by Robert and three others. Robert chose to pray for Matt, asking God to "help him through his struggles and make this upcoming week one where he glorifies You with his actions."

After the devotional was over, Matt found himself getting hugged a lot by people on the team. Several said they'd continue to pray for him. His mom held him tightly and said she was proud of him for speaking up. His dad's hug was briefer but no less heartfelt.

Matt wasn't sure his attitude had changed But he knew that he felt better for having asked for prayers. Maybe with a lot of people talking to God about it something would happen.

Maybe he would wake up tomorrow with a brand-new attitude. Matt prayed that would be the case.

- TWENTY-FIVE -

MATT WOKE UP THE NEXT MORNING with his stomach roiling. He lay in bed a moment, watching the room spin lazily around him. *Oh, no…*

Throwing his covers off, he staggered out of bed and barely got to the bathroom in time before he emptied the contents of his stomach into the toilet bowl.

Robert came into the bathroom, his eyes wide. "Oh, man, you're sick?"

Matt opened his mouth to answer and found himself retching again. Robert hovered over him, his face anxious.

Once Matt was finished he weakly sat back against the cool tile wall. He stomach ached and the taste in his mouth was foul. "Ugh," he groaned.

"You want me to get your dad?" Robert asked.

Matt nodded, afraid to open his mouth again. Robert turned and hurried out of the bathroom, leaving Matt alone in his misery.

It didn't take long before his parents were in the room. His dad crouched down in front of him. "Okay, Matt. Tell me how you're feeling."

"Stomach hurts," Matt rasped, his throat sore from vomiting. "I'm a little dizzy and I feel hot."

His dad examined him as he sat on the cold bathroom floor, feeling his head and gently palpating his stomach. "Well, I think you caught your mom's bug, son. Can you stand up?"

Matt let his dad help him get to his feet. He staggered to the sink and rinsed out his mouth with bottled water. "So now what?"

"I think you can go back to bed," his dad said. "I have some medicine that will help with your symptoms, but it will probably have a sedating effect."

Matt groaned, but he had to admit the idea of bed sounded good at the moment. He let his father put an arm around him and help him make the short trip back to his cot.

Robert was standing near the door. "Anything I can do to help?"

"Yes," Matt's dad said. "Go downstairs and get me three or four bottles of water from the dining room. Let Stan know Matt's ill and won't be going to the site today."

Matt's mom sat on the cot and placed a cool hand on his forehead. "How about I bring our laptop in here? That way when you feel better you'll have something fun to do."

"Thanks, Mom," Matt said. His dad left with her and Matt was left alone for a moment. He felt frustrated. He'd been praying to God for a change in his attitude, and this was his answer? He got sick?

Robert came back first with the water. "Stan says a half-dozen people are down with this thing," he told Matt as he lined the water bottles on the table. "He's really worried."

Matt gave Robert a wry grin. "Should I still thank God for my health?"

Robert grimaced. "Well, it could be worse."

Before Matt could come up with a proper retort his parents arrived with the laptop and medicine.

Matt's dad looked a little harried. "It seems you're not the only one down with this," he told Matt. "Take the medicine and make sure you stay hydrated today. I want at least three of those bottles emptied by the time we get back, more if you can manage it."

Matt swallowed the small pill his father gave him and washed it down with a swig of water. "Do I have to stay in bed?"

"Not unless you want to," his father told him. "You might want to rest for now and get up a little later." He squeezed his son's shoulder. "I have to talk to the other doctors about this and see what we can do for the others. I'll look in on you when we get back."

His mom kissed him on the cheek. "I know you feel terrible, but it seems to just be a 24-hour thing. Do what your dad said and you'll be fine."

Robert grinned and waved at him from across the room. "No offense, but I'm going to stay away from you for the moment. I don't want to catch this!"

"Ha, ha," Matt said. "Thanks for the water."

"No problem," Robert said. "I'm going to get ready to get some breakfast. You need the bathroom again?"

"Ugh, don't mention food or I might," Matt protested, pressing a hand to his stomach.

"Sorry," Robert said. He grabbed his things and went into the bathroom, leaving Matt alone again.

Matt lay on the cot feeling sorry for himself. He felt awful, to be honest. It wasn't bad enough that he was in a third world country. No, now he had to be sick, too.

He rolled over on his side and stared at the wall. What else could go wrong on this trip?

* * *

When Matt woke up two hours later, he felt a little better. His stomach seemed to have settled down, though he felt drained of energy. Remembering his father's instructions, he opened up a fresh water bottle and drank half of it down.

He sat down at the small table or desk and turned on his parents' laptop. While it booted up he sipped a little more water, feeling his head start to clear. Soon the computer was up and running and Matt was on the Internet.

He checked his email, surprised at how much junk email had accumulated in his box. After that he cruised Facebook, catching up on his friends' doings.

Matt thought about posting something about Guyana, something like, "Stuck here and sick. Wish I was home." He decided against it. His mom had a Facebook account and he knew she'd see it for sure. Matt didn't need that kind of trouble.

Suddenly he remembered that his folks had installed the communication program Skype on the laptop. He checked the laptop's carrying case and found a set of headsets with a microphone attached.

Matt quickly signed onto his Skype account. He wondered if it would work here in Guyana. Then he remembered someone – Robert he thought – saying Harry used Skype to talk to people in the states.

Clay was online. Matt decided to give his friend a call. He selected the green "video call" button and waited.

Clay answered quickly and in seconds Matt was staring at his friend's round face. "Matt? That you? For real?"

Matt grinned. "Yep. All the way from Guyana. How about that?"

"Wow. That's, I mean, that's amazing. I'm actually talking to you while you're in another country."

"Yeah, it's pretty cool," Matt agreed.

"So how come you're calling me? Aren't you supposed to be doing something?" Clay asked.

Matt grimaced. "I'm sick. There's a stupid stomach flu going around and I caught it."

"Oh, man, that stinks!" Clay said. "You sure it's stomach flu? Maybe you caught some weird jungle disease."

"It's not some weird jungle disease," Matt said, rolling his eyes. "My mom had it yesterday, and she's fine today."

"Well okay," Clay said. "So, how bad is it? I mean, is it totally primitive?"

"Well, they obviously have internet access," Matt said. "And air conditioning in the room."

"That sounds good," Clay said. "You sharing a room with your parents?"

"Nope," Matt said. "Robert Price."

"Oh, you've got to be kidding me!" Clay howled with laughter. "You're stuck with Righteous Robert? Man, you must be having an awful time!"

"It's . . . " Matt hesitated. "He's been okay, for the most part."

"Oh, I bet," Clay chuckled. "Come on, you haven't wanted to smack him even once? He acts so goody-goody, maybe that's what made you sick!"

Matt was uncomfortable, and it wasn't the virus. He and Clay laughed at Robert all the time, calling him "Righteous Robert" behind his back and stuff.

But the preacher's kid had been nice to Matt, even tried to help him. Matt realized his opinion of Robert had changed to a certain extent during the week.

"Earth to Matt, Earth to Matt," Clay chanted. "You still there?"

"Yeah," Matt said. He decided to change the subject. "It's really hot here. And I have a million mosquito bites."

"I bet," Clay said. "You having to help take care of any sick people?"

"No," Matt said. "I helped out with the kids, mostly. One time I sat in on some Bible studies."

"You got stuck with the kids? Man, you must've hated that. What about the Bible studies? Totally boring, right?"

"No, the studies were interesting," Matt said. "But yeah, watching the kids got old after a bit."

"Man, if I were in your place, I'd be in like a total sulk the whole time!" Clay said. "And you got what, another week?"

"Yeah," Matt said. "But I'm trying to have a better attitude. Sulking hasn't been working so well."

"Right," Clay chuckled. "Just don't become a goody-goody on me, okay? Do what you have to to get through the week, but don't change who you are, man."

Matt felt his stomach twist. "Hey, I'm gonna sign off for now, okay? I'm feeling a little sick."

"Ugh. Sure, call me later if you get a chance," Clay said.

Matt signed off and stared at the computer screen. The call hadn't made him feel at all better – in fact, he felt worse.

"Don't change who you are," Clay had said.

But what if that was what he had to do?

- TWENTY-SIX -

MATT GOT UP from the computer and made his way to the balcony. He let the hot breeze fan his face as he leaned on the railing and looked up at the cloudy sky. It looked like it was going to rain.

He was confused. He'd been trying to do what was right, and he still felt lousy. Why was it so hard? Why couldn't he just turn himself around?

He thought he was a pretty good guy. Sure, he sinned, but he didn't do any of the big no-nos. He did a lot better than a lot of his friends at school.

So why did he suddenly feel it wasn't enough?

There was a knock in the door. Wondering who might be coming to see him – maybe another sick team member? – Matt opened the door.

Anil stood there, a huge grin on his face. "Matt! Good, you are out of bed."

Matt blinked. "What are you doing here?":

"I have come to visit you. Your father told me you were sick," Anil said. "I wanted to see how you were doing."

Matt shrugged. "I feel lousy. But I guess I'm gonna live."

Anil studied him. "You do look a little pale. Maybe you should sit down?"

Matt saw that Anil wasn't leaving, so he gestured for him to enter the room. Matt sank down on the bed and let Anil take the desk chair.

"Aren't you afraid of catching this?" Matt asked. He took a gulp of water the bottle in his hand.

"I am tough. Besides, we are told to visit the sick," Anil said. "I will take my chances with you."

Matt snorted. "I'm not great company at the moment. No offense."

"I am not offended," Anil assured him. "But I am curious. Besides being sick, how are you feeling?"

"Look, I'm not in the mood for a lecture," Matt said, closing his eyes.

"I am not trying to lecture you. I just wondered how you were doing."

Matt didn't answer at once. "I dunno," he finally admitted. He opened his eyes and looked over at Anil. "I'm doing a lot of thinking."

Anil nodded. "Thinking is good. Tell me, what are you thinking about?"

"Stuff," Matt said. "About what I need to do – wondering how to make this week better."

"You have been praying about it?" Anil asked.

"Yeah, and see what happened? I got sick," Matt said with a bitter laugh.

Anil shook his head. "You are not looking at this right." He looked around the cluttered room. "Why don't you come with me and sit outside? The fresh air will do you good."

"What good will that do?" Matt asked.

"I thought it would be more pleasant than being stuck in a cold room," Anil answered with a shiver.

"It feels cold to you?" Matt asked. The room was comfortable to him – if anything, it was almost too warm.

"I am used to my country's weather," Anil reminded him. "But come. Bring some water to drink. After a bit, we can have lunch."

"Uh, no offense, but food still doesn't sound good to me right now," Matt said, his stomach twinging at the thought.

"Perhaps we can find something that will sit well with you," Anil said. "Unless you simply want to be alone and feel bad."

Matt glared at Anil. "You're not going to give up until I give in, are you?"

Anil smiled. "Steve tells me I can be very stubborn."

"Fine," Matt said. "Let's go." He got up and grabbed a full bottle of water and followed Anil downstairs.

The air was heavy with humidity. The clouds had a weighty look to them, as if they couldn't wait to dump their rain on the earth. Matt and Anil grabbed a couple of plastic chairs and sat a little away from the pool.

In spite of the heat, Matt had to admit he felt a little better with some fresh air on his face. The two of them sat quietly for a while, each with his own thoughts.

Matt decided to ask Anil a question. "Why do you want to be a gospel preacher?"

Anil thought a moment before giving his answer. "I have given it a lot of thought. It is the greatest thing I could do for others, teaching them about the good news about Jesus. Many Guyanese still need the message, and they need people to bring it to them."

"But you could do that and do something else, couldn't you?"

"I could," Anil said. "But I do not want to do anything else. What about you, Matt? What would you like to do with your life?"

"I don't know," Matt admitted. "I like computers, and I've thought about learning to make video games."

"You do not want to be a doctor, like your father?" Anil asked.

Matt looked at the clear waters of the pool. "No. People think doctors have a great life, but he has to work really hard. And I don't think I'd be good with patients, either."

"It is hard work to become a doctor, yes? A lot of studying."

Matt grinned. "That's true too. I'm not interested in spending eight more years in school."

Anil smiled back. "I understand that feeling. I have to study hard to be a preacher. I hope to be a good one."

Matt considered that. "I think you'll be a good one. Your sermon was okay, even if you were trying to skewer me."

"Not only you – do you think you are the only one to struggle with a bad attitude?" Anil retorted. "It is a common problem, I assure you."

"I guess," Matt said. "No one else here seems to be dealing with it."

"You are too concerned with thinking about yourself and your problems," Anil told him. "You should think of others, too."

Matt felt a drop of water hit his cheek. He saw rain begin to patter on the surface of the pool. "We should go inside."

The two of them ran for the inside of the hotel, along with the few other people that had been outside. The rain became heavy, obscuring the view of outside.

It was early for lunch, but Anil and Matt decided to go into the dining room anyway. He noticed Brad and Susie were there, nursing cups of hot tea, and he waved to them.

Matt thought he might be able to handle something light and asked the waitress for a suggestion. The waitress recommended tea, toast, and Jell-O. Matt decided to try those things out. Anil ordered a chicken sandwich with fries. The waiterss wrote down their orders and headed to another table.

While they waited for their food, Anil asked, "How is your attitude coming?"

Matt toyed with his silverware. "It's hard. And I don't think I'm doing it right."

Anil said nothing, just waited for Matt to go on. Matt took a deep breath. "I mean, I'm trying, okay? I've gotten advice from people. I've been praying. But right now I just want to be grumpy about being stuck here."

"You are sick. That is understandable," Anil said.

"But I feel like everyone wants me to be different than what I am. Like I'm not good enough."

Anil shrugged. "None of us are good enough. That is why we need the gospel."

"I don't mean like that," Matt argued. "I mean they want me to be someone I'm not. Someone like Robert."

"Who is Robert?"

"My roommate," Matt sighed. "He's always so good and everything. Like he's holy or something. He's like every parent's dream of what they want their kid to be."

Anil shook his head. "I have not seen someone like that here. You all seem like regular people to me."

Matt paused while the waitress served them their drinks. He stirred some of the brownish sugar in his tea. "It's just that – I'm not like that. I'm me. But here I feel like I'm supposed to be someone else."

"You will always be you, Matt, even if you do what is right," Anil pointed out. He sipped his cola. "Are you normally grumpy and angry?"

"No."

"Yet you have been so here," Anil said. "So are you being someone else already?"

Matt frowned. "I . . . that's not what I meant."

"Then what did you mean?"

Matt was saved from having to answer right away by Susie and Brad coming to their table. The three of them compared symptoms and agreed that getting sick was no picnic. Anil joined in the conversation and they made small talk until Matt's and Anil's lunch arrived.

After Brad and Susie left, Matt dug into his orange Jell-O, hoping Anil had forgotten his question. "So, will Steve Lockwood be mad that you're spending so much time with me?"

"He understands," Anil said. "And I think I understand you too, Matt. You are afraid to change, because it might turn you into someone you do not wish to be. Is this correct?"

Matt swallowed his spoonful of Jell-O. "I do want a good attitude. I don't want to feel mad the rest of the trip."

"But are you willing to do what you need to do?" Anil asked.

"What do I need to do?" Matt said, feeling annoyed. "I'm trying. I'm praying. I'm even looking for reasons to be thankful. But I still have these feelings."

"Do not let your feelings rule your behavior," Anil suggested. "Decide you will act differently from your feelings."

"But then I'll still be feeling bad."

"Perhaps not. Perhaps when you act differently the feelings will change to match your actions."

"Hm," Matt said, munching on a triangle of toast. "So just do it?"

"Do what you have been doing, but decide to act despite your feelings," Anil said. He wiped his mouth with his napkin. "You are already more than halfway through your trip. You have already started to change. Just continue."

"I have?" Matt asked.

"You are taking advice. Your attitude has been improved, though you know you can do even better. And," Anil said with a twinkle in his eye, "you did not throw me out of your room this morning. So I would say your attitude is better."

Matt chuckled. "Thanks."

They spent the remainder of lunch talking about movies they'd both seen. Matt found out they had similar tastes in movies, both agreeing that the "Twilight" series was not for them.

By the time lunch was finished, Matt was feeling tired. He told Anil he was going up to his room for a nap. Anil walked with him to his room and told him he hoped he felt better.

Matt lay on his cot and thought about everything. He rolled over and grabbed his list of things to be thankful for.

Might as well try again, he thought. Opening the piece of paper so he could read what was written there, he began to pray.

- TWENTY-SEVEN -

S TAN LOOKED CONCERNED as he stood in front of the team with Steve Lockwood. "We have a problem."

Matt, in his customary chair near the back, was forced to agree. He was feeling a lot better than he had in the morning. The same couldn't be said of everybody.

Two more team members had come down with the stomach virus while on the site. Those who had not yet caught it were nervous, wondering if they would be next.

"It looks like this is going to run through the team," Lockwood said. "Hopefully no more doctors will come down with it – but there's no guarantees."

Matt glanced over at his dad. He'd been one of the two to get hit with the virus while at the site, but had insisted on continuing to work. Now he looked pale and shaky.

"The doctors have medicine for those of you still suffering from this," Stan said. "In the meantime, they reinforce that you need to wash your hands frequently and remain hydrated. Those of you who have this, refrain from physical contact with others if possible. We're trying to limit this virus as much as we can."

Matt thought of Anil as he tipped back his chair. He'd spent a lot of time with him today. Hopefully he wouldn't come down with this illness as a result.

"Those of you without specific assignments need to be flexible – we're probably going to be moving you around over the next few days to different jobs. Please be willing to serve."

"Now we'd like to offer up a prayer for the team," Lockwood said. "Satan can use this to discourage you, and we don't want that to happen. You've done good work thus far: let's pray you can keep it up for the rest of the week."

Matt bowed his head as Lockwood prayed. He thought about his own prayer earlier, about doing better. It looked like his resolve would be put to the test, given what was going on with the team.

After the group was dismissed Matt checked on his dad. "I'll be fine," his dad said, with an attempt at a smile. "You get your rest. You'll be needed tomorrow."

Matt saw Jenna talking with Susie. He wished he could just walk up to her and start talking. But he felt awkward still. Especially with how he'd been acting.

She caught him looking at him and after saying one last thing to Susie, walked over to him. "Barry missed you today."

"He did?" Matt asked, surprised.

Jenna smiled. "He kept asking, 'Where is that boy with the funny faces?' He wasn't happy at all."

"Oh," Matt said. He found that his dirty sneakers were suddenly very interesting. "Well, um, I should be there tomorrow. I feel a lot better."

"That's good," Jenna said. "Well, I guess I'll see you tomorrow."

"Yeah," Matt said, still looking at his shoes. He could see Jenna's pink sneakers move away, and he mentally kicked himself for being so shy around her.

Frustrated, he headed back to his room. Robert was already there sitting on his cot, reading his Bible. "How're you feeling, Matt?"

"Fine," Matt answered. "I should be able to go to the site tomorrow."

"Great," Robert said. "I hope I don't catch this. Maybe it's done with the team."

"I'll try not to breathe on you," Matt grumped, heading to his cot.

"Hey, man, I didn't mean it like that," Robert said, straightening up.

"Okay, whatever," Matt said. He was tired and still thinking about Jenna. He pulled off his shirt and tossed it into his suitcase.

Robert looked like he wanted to say something else, but instead he sighed and went back to his Bible.

Matt felt a twinge of guilt – none of what he was feeling was Robert's fault – but he didn't feel up to setting things right. So he continued getting ready for bed, wondering what the next day would hold for the team.

* * *

Matt woke up to hear Robert in the bathroom. He closed his eyes. *Poor Robert. Looked like he caught the bug after all.*

He felt some sympathy for his roommate and decided to throw some clothes on and let his father know that he had another patient.

After pulling on a t-shirt and a pair of pants he called into the bathroom, "I'm gonna get my dad, okay?"

A groan was Robert's only response. Matt felt his own stomach churn in sympathy and he decided to leave the room before he risked a relapse.

His mother answered the door, dressed in a blue silk bathrobe. "Robert's sick," Matt said. "I thought I should let Dad know."

"Your father is with the Trasks…it looks like they came down with this virus as well," his mother sighed.

"Jenna's sick again?" Matt asked.

"No, I think she's fine. I think it's just her parents," his mother answered. "Why don't you go downstairs and grab some water for Robert, and I'll let your dad know about him when he gets back to the room."

Matt went down to the dining room and waited in line with others from the team to get some bottled water. People were talking about the virus and how it had gotten to more people, and wondering if they were going to be able to manage on site that day.

Matt wondered that himself. He got his water bottles, charging them to the room. When he returned he found Robert sprawled out on his cot, an arm thrown over his eyes.

Seeing his roommate look so pitiful caused a stab of guilt in Matt. "Sorry, man, guess I gave you this."

"It might not have been you," Robert croaked. "What did your dad say?"

"He wasn't in the room, the Trasks are down with this too." Matt put the water bottles on the desk and offered one to Robert. "You feel like drinking some water?"

"I dunno, I feel awful," Robert said. He moved his arm so he could look at Matt. "Thanks, though."

Matt shrugged. "I'll leave it by the bed here." He decided to grab his shower and get ready to go. No way he was staying here if he could help it.

In the shower Matt wondered about how the virus was hampering the team. Why would God allow that? Wasn't He happy with what they were doing? Didn't He want the trip to succeed?

He felt his mind running in circles with the questions. By the time he got dressed and left the bathroom, he still didn't have any answers.

Matt's father arrived as Matt was packing up his backpack. He gave Robert some medicine and told him to rest and remain hydrated. The doctor still looked pale but not quite as sick as he had the night before.

"Dad, are you staying here?" Matt asked as soon as his father finished with Robert.

His father shook his head. "They need all the doctors on site, Matt. I'm going to go."

Matt frowned. "You haven't gotten that much rest," he pointed out.

"I've gotten enough," his father said. "I'll be taking fewer patients, but I can't just stop, son." He put a hand on Matt's shoulder. "I'll be fine. How about you? Do you feel up to going?"

Matt nodded. "I'm tired, but I can handle it. I don't want to stay here anyway."

"All right," his dad said. "Don't eat anything too heavy for breakfast – you don't want a relapse. I know Stan will appreciate your being there, we're going to be short-handed."

Matt followed his father out of the room. He headed downstairs to the dining room again, noting several empty places at the tables. His dad hadn't been kidding – they were going to be short-handed. A very harried looking Stan was sitting with Steve Lockwood, talking urgently.

Well, he thought, *I wanted to try to have a better attitude. Guess this is as good a place to start as any.* Hoping he wouldn't regret it, he walked over to where the two men sat.

Stan looked up. "Matt. How are you feeling?"

"Better," Matt said. "I just wanted you to know that I'll do whatever you need me to do today." He grinned slightly. "Except be a doctor. I don't think I have the skills for that."

"I appreciate that," Stan said, smiling a little at Matt's stab at humor. "I'll let you know what I need from you when we get there, all right?"

"Sure," Matt said. Feeling as if he'd done his part, he went to grab some eggs and toast.

As he sat with his mother and started eating, he wondered what task he'd be saddled with that day. And just how badly his new resolve would be tested.

- TWENTY-EIGHT -

ANIL SMILED AS MATT made his way to his van. "Matt! You are feeling better?"

"Yeah," Matt nodded. "But a lot of the team is sick."

The Guyanese man's smile faded. "I know. I have been praying for you all. This is not good."

"Why is God letting it happen?" Matt asked. He still didn't have an answer to that question and hoped maybe Anil could solve it for him.

Instead, Anil shrugged. "I do not know. God's ways are not ours. I do not believe He afflicted you with this illness, though."

"But He could've stopped it," Matt insisted.

"He could stop a number of things," Anil pointed out. "But He chooses to let some things occur. Things far worse than a stomach virus."

That was true. But the answer didn't satisfy Matt. In fact, it troubled him even more.

He thought about it all the way to the clinic site. Anil was right – God permitted all kinds of bad things to happen in the world. Yet He had the power to make it all stop. Why didn't He? What purpose was there in allowing such things to go on?

Matt was so lost in thought he didn't realize they'd arrived at the site until Anil called his name. Blinking, he saw others getting out of the van and hurried to catch up with everyone.

Stan was rushing about, talking to people and checking to see who had made it out. Matt hung out in the auditorium, not sure what to do. He saw Jenna gathering the kids together and waved to Barry, who grinned and waved back.

Finally Stan came up to Matt. "Do you know any first aid?" he asked.

The question caught Matt by surprise. "Yeah, they taught it in Scouts. I remember some of it."

"Okay," Stan said. "I have Gladys starting off teaching the first aid course we've put together here. If you watched her for a couple of sessions, do you think you could do it so I could use her with the doctors?"

Gladys was one of the nurses on the team. Matt remembered that. He felt nervous – this sounded like a big responsibility. "Stan, I don't know. Like I said, I remember some of the stuff from Scouts, but not all of it."

"It's mostly on a flip chart," Stan assured him. "Please Matt, would you at least give it a try? I need Gladys with the doctors as soon as possible and I'm running out of people to use."

Matt sighed. He really didn't want to do it, but wasn't part of a good attitude doing what you didn't want to do? "Sure Stan, I'll give it a shot."

"Thanks," Stan said. "Go ahead and talk to Gladys, I'm sure you'll do fine."

Matt sought out the nurse. He found her setting up a flip chart on an easel in front of a set of about fifteen chairs.

"Stan sent me to help you," he told the gray-haired woman.

She smiled at him, blue eyes twinkling behind her glasses. "So nice of Stan to send a handsome young man to give me a hand."

Matt blushed. "I – I'm supposed to watch you a couple of times then try to do it myself."

"You'll do fine," she said, patting his arm. "The class practically teaches itself. I'll make sure you're comfortable with it before I leave you alone."

"Thanks," Matt said. He looked at the flip chart, which was apparently homemade. It consisted of a number of pages written and drawn in colorful magic marker. To his relief, a lot of it was common sense things that he already knew.

Before long the group was gathered in a circle in the auditorium for their customary prayer before opening. Matt sent up a private prayer himself – *please don't let me screw up too badly.*

After the prayer, he went with Gladys to wait for their first group. "They may have questions," she told him. "'I don't know' is a perfectly good answer, and you can suggest they ask a nurse or a doctor when they see them."

Matt nodded, feeling his mouth grow dry. This was different from playing with the kids, which suddenly didn't seem to be such a bad job. "What if I screw up?" he asked.

Gladys smiled. "You'll do fine," she assured him. "Here, let's quickly go over the chart while we wait."

By the time the first group was seated, Matt felt a little better. Gladys had answered the few questions he'd had and now he simply had to stand back and watch her teach.

She smiled at the group. "Good afternoon. My name is Gladys and this handsome young man here is my helper, Matt."

He managed a half-hearted wave at the group of women who looked at him and then returned their attention to Gladys.

She went through the flip chart, explaining the tips on each page. At one point she used Matt to demonstrate how to treat a cut. "Let's say it's on his arm," she said, pressing two fingers on Matt's forearm. "You put pressure on the wound and raise it up above his heart to stop the bleeding."

The group was attentive and silent for the presentation. There were a few questions, and Gladys answered them without hesitation. Matt was relieved to hear that the questions were pretty basic and ones he could've answered himself.

He watched Gladys go through the routine with a second group. Once they left, she turned to him. "All right, it's your turn. I'll stay and watch, but I think you'll do just fine."

Matt gulped, but nodded. "Okay."

By the time the next group was seated his mouth was dry. He took a swallow of water and then stood by the flip chart, wondering if people could hear his heart hammering in his chest. "Um . . . hi. My name is Matt, and this is Gladys, and, um, we're going to talk to you about some basic first aid."

He stumbled through the presentation, leaning heavily on the fact Gladys would be there to correct any mistakes he made. Despite his nervousness he managed to finish it up with no major errors. One woman had a question that Gladys had to answer, but besides that it didn't go too badly.

"You look like you have it well in hand," Gladys smiled as the group filed out of the area. "I think I'd best go help out the doctors now."

Matt tried to quell the panic that rose in him. "Couldn't you stay for one more session?" he asked, trying to keep the whining tone out of his voice.

"The doctors need me, Matt," Gladys said. "You're going to be fine. Just follow the flip chart and be pleasant. That's all you need to do."

She squeezed his arm and headed into the building, leaving Matt to face the chairs filling with men and women alone. He saw his hand was shaking as he brought his water bottle to his lips. Why had she left him? He wasn't ready!

The group sat silently, waiting for him to speak. Matt took one more swallow of water and then replaced the bottle in its holster on his waistpack. He cleared his throat and began to speak.

To his surprise, the session went well. No one had any questions he couldn't answer and they listened attentively during his presentation. Matt felt his stomach unclench slightly. Maybe he could do this.

He lost count of the number of groups that went through. Each time the lesson became more and more automatic for him. He even managed to insert a few jokes into the presentation, which got a few chuckles from his audience.

When Gladys came back to relieve him for a break, he was surprised at the amount of time that had passed. Matt headed for the break room and sat, his trembling legs telling him he'd been standing for quite a while. He dug into his backpack for a can of spaghetti and meatballs and a spoon.

Dr. Lopez was just finishing up his own cold meal when Matt arrived. He nodded to the young man. "How are you doing?"

"Fine," Matt said. He didn't know the doctor very well, but remembered he'd been sick on Sunday. "Are you feeling better?"

"Yes," he said. "And you? Were you not sick as well?"

"Yeah, I'm feeling okay," Matt said. He grimaced as he spooned up some of his canned food. "Is this your first time in Guyana?"

"No," Dr. Lopez said. "I have been coming here the past three years. It is a good work, and I am honored to be a part of it."

"It's my first time," Matt admitted.

"I know," the doctor said. "Your father is a good doctor, a hard worker. I am glad you decided to come."

Matt scowled into his food. He still wasn't sure he was glad about being here. But he didn't want to say that to the doctor. Instead, he replied, "Thanks. My dad is a good doctor."

Dr. Lopez smiled. He tossed his empty can into the trash and stood. "I hope your family will return next year. Guyana needs workers like you."

Matt was too startled to answer as the doctor left. Return next year? Part of him was still counting the days until he left the country. Coming back again? He couldn't even imagine it.

Sure, today was going all right, but that still didn't change the facts. Did it?

Confused, Matt ate the rest of his food without tasting it. He wasn't sure what he thought any more.

And that bothered him more than he could say.

- TWENTY-NINE -

WITH A SIGH OF RELIEF, Matt dropped into one of the empty chairs after the final group left. He glanced over at the flip chart, wondering if he'd ever be able to forget it after going through it time and again.

Stan drifted over and sat down next to him. "You doing all right, Matt?"

Matt ran a hand through his hair. "I think so. Just really tired."

"Thanks for doing this," Stan told him. "With us so shorthanded, we needed everyone to be flexible."

"It's okay," Matt shrugged. He yawned. "I hope I can stay awake through the service tonight."

"I wanted to ask you about that," Stan said. "Would you be willing to lead a prayer at the service? Opening or closing prayer, I don't care which."

Matt blinked, surprised and a little unnerved. "You sure about that? I mean, you really want me to lead a prayer?"

"Why not?" Stan asked.

"Well," Matt said. "I mean, I'm trying to do better, you know? But after last week, I figured . . . "

Stan waved a hand. "Last week was last week. You're trying, as you said. That counts for something." He looked Matt in the eye. "So, can you lead a prayer?"

Matt shifted in his chair. He'd led prayers at home, but this felt different, more scary. "I...I guess."

"Good," Stan clapped his shoulder and stood. "We'll be setting up before too long for the service, could use your help."

"Yeah, sure," Matt said. He didn't get up right away. His legs were a little rubbery from all the standing he'd done and he wanted a moment's more rest before he started moving benches again.

He tilted his head back and closed his eyes. His thoughts bounced around his head like pinballs. It would be easy to doze off here, despite the heat and the itching on his arms from all his bug bites.

Matt was confused. He didn't want to be here, did he? He hated it here. Didn't he? Or was the country starting to get to him, in some kind of insidious way? Was he changing, like he prayed for? And was it a good thing?

"Hey."

Matt opened one eye to see Barry staring at him. The little boy started to grin at him and then pulled an exaggerated frown.

Matt sighed. "Okay, buddy, let's do this." He made a face at the scowling child. "Don't smile, remember?"

It didn't take long before Barry was dissolved in giggles and Matt was forced to grin back. He straightened up in his chair, wiping the sweat off his face. He shoved his conflicting thoughts into the back of his mind for the time being.

At least entertaining a child was something he understood.

* * *

". . . In Jesus' name, amen."

Matt finished off the closing prayer and the congregation echoed the "amen." He took a deep breath, glad that he'd managed to utter the prayer without his voice shaking.

He looked over the sea of dark and light faces. He mom gave him an encouraging smile before turning to talk to a woman seated behind her. Matt stepped forward, only to be stopped by an old woman who sat in the front row.

Her wrinkled face lit up as she spoke to him. "That was a good prayer. Praying to God is always a good thing."

He ducked his head. "Thanks, ma'am."

She laid a hand on his arm. "I am so glad you and your people are here," she continued. "You bring us the word of God, which is my food."

Matt felt embarrassed. "Um, you're welcome, ma'am."

"God will bless you for what you do here," she told him. "I pray for your people every day, that God will be with you."

Matt nodded, then was relieved when Harry came up. "Good evening, sister Frances," he said, taking her hand. "How are you feeling tonight?"

She turned to speak to Harry and Matt used the opportunity to slip away. He found he was uncomfortable with the woman's gratitude, given his feelings about her country.

He was complimented by several others on his prayer. Matt thanked them, though he didn't think his prayer was anything special. He said as much to Anil when he got into the van later that evening.

"You never know," Anil said. "You may have said something that touched someone's heart. God may have used you despite what you think."

Matt wasn't sure he bought that. "Why would God use me, when I'm such a mess?"

Anil laughed as he passed a slower moving vehicle. "It doesn't matter if you are, as you say, a 'mess.' God always uses imperfect people – that is all He has to work with, after all."

Matt gulped as Anil swung back into their lane, barely missing the bumper of a car ahead of them. "Everyone else seems to be doing better than me."

"Everyone else has struggles, same as you. Not in the same way, but we all have things we are dealing with," Anil said.

Matt thought about that the rest of the way back to the hotel. Once there, he lingered by the van until everyone had gotten out. Once he and Anil had some privacy, he said, "I don't think anyone else here resents coming. I still do. What do I do about that?"

Anil shrugged. "You have to stop looking at the bad. What good have you found here? Things you would have missed. Like the falls."

"No offense?" Matt said. "The falls were great, but they aren't enough."

Anil leaned against the van. "I understand that. But it is a start. Good has come from this trip. Many sick have been helped. Many have heard the gospel. Some have even responded."

"That would've happened whether I came or not," Matt said.

"But you are here and a part of it. Do not discount that."

Matt folded his arms and leaned on the van next to Anil. He looked up at the dark sky high above the hotel. "But it doesn't matter that I'm here. Others are doing it all."

"Then make it matter," Anil persisted. "You think you are nothing, just a teenager with a bad attitude. There is more to you than that, Matt. Find it, and you will matter. Believe me."

Matt's stomach chose that moment to rumble. He straightened up. "I guess I better go catch some dinner. Thanks for the chat."

"I will be here again tomorrow," Anil promised. "Do not worry. You have already grown much in your time here. Just a little bit more and the resentment you feel will melt like snow in Guyana."

Matt raised his eyebrows. "Have you ever seen snow, Anil?"

The young man laughed. "No, of course not. But you must agree it would not last long in my country."

Matt grinned. "I guess you have me there. See you tomorrow."

Before going to the dining room, Matt decided to check on Robert. He found his roommate sitting on his cot, an open Bible in his lap.

"How're you feeling?" Matt asked.

Robert grimaced. "Feels like something tried to kick its way out of my stomach, but other than that, a little better."

"Yeah, I felt that way yesterday myself," Matt said. "Want me to bring you something?"

"Naw, I'm good, thanks anyway," Robert said. "I had some tea before, and I'm trying to drink a lot of water."

"Okay," Matt said. He headed back downstairs to get his own dinner, feeling like he'd done something right.

Of course, anyone could've checked on Robert. And a couple of days ago Matt wouldn't have bothered to do it.

But maybe it was a start. To what, Matt wasn't sure. As he got in line for dinner he decided all he could do was keep trying and see where it led.

Maybe it would be something good.

- THIRTY -

Hey ROBERT," Matt said as the boys were getting ready the next morning, "If Stan says okay, can I sit in with you on some Bible studies again?"

"Sure," Robert said, looking surprised. "If Stan okays it, I have no problem with it. If I'm even doing Bible studies today I might not be."

Matt frowned. "Because people are sick?"

"Yeah," Robert said. "Though maybe this virus is finally through with us. That would be a blessing."

"Yeah, I can't argue with that," Matt said. He shrugged on his backpack. "I'm gonna get some breakfast. You coming?"

"Yeah," Robert said. "Man, I thought I'd never want to even look at food again yesterday."

Matt grinned. "Boy, I know what you mean."

Matt sought out Stan at breakfast and asked about sitting in on the Bible studies. Stan thought about it for a moment. "I'd really like you back at teaching first aid, if you don't mind, Matt. Maybe later today I can switch you out, but Gladys said you did a super job and I really need her back with the doctors."

"But she's been teaching it right along," Matt said. "Can't she keep doing it?"

"We're seeing a lot of people this week, Matt. More than last week," Stan explained. "I need all the medical people I can get. I'll try to cycle someone else in there later, but I really need you starting it off."

"Fine," Matt sighed. He knew he sounded sulky but he didn't care. He turned from Stan and went to grab some breakfast, his earlier good mood gone.

He'd thought he'd figured things out. It occurred to him that the biggest difference he could make was in the Bible studies. He thought that leading someone to Christ would be something he could do – with Robert's help, of course.

He set his plate full of food down with a thud. Well, so much for that idea. He guessed that teaching first aid was important in its own way. But it wasn't what he wanted to do.

"Everything all right, Matt?" his mother asked.

He thought about not answering, but knew that would lead to more questions. "It's okay," he muttered, forking up some scrambled eggs.

"Are you sure?" his dad asked. Dr. Brooks looked a lot better than he had yesterday. "You look like a storm cloud."

Matt swallowed his mouthful of food. "I just asked Stan if I could sit in on some Bible studies and he said no. I have to teach first aid again."

"Well, I know you're disappointed, but we really need all hands on deck. We still have a few people out sick, though praise God it isn't more," his dad offered.

"Yeah, Stan told me," Matt grumbled.

"How many sick today?" his mom asked.

"Only three," his dad answered. "Unfortunately, Dick Nelson is one of them. He says he'll come work, but I remember what that was like. The rest of us doctors will be picking up the slack."

Matt tuned out his parent's conversation. He instead stewed. *This isn't fair. I'm trying, I want to do something important, and I get stuck with a lousy first aid course!*

In every thing give thanks: for this is the will of God in Christ Jesus concerning you.

Matt almost dropped his fork. He remembered Robert had quoted this verse to him a few days ago when he'd tried to encourage Matt to be more thankful.

Now the verse was back in his head. Was God trying to tell him something?

Matt thought about it. Could he be thankful he was teaching the first aid class? He was rather ticked off about it, to be honest. How could he thank God for it?

He finished breakfast without a concrete answer. Frustrated, and more than a little crabby, he headed out to wait for the vans.

* * *

"And, um, that's the end of the course. Any questions?"

Matt was relieved that this group didn't seem to have anything to ask. He directed them to a waiting area and took a gulp of water while waiting for his next group.

He could see the Bible study area from where he stood. Robert, his mom, and several others were busy teaching God's word. Here he was, teaching people to wash their hands and what to do in cases of accidents.

His legs ached from standing so much. It was sweltering, his shirt stuck to his body, and he slapped away a mosquito that tried to feast on his arm.

Maybe after this group he could get a break. The day was almost half over, and the makeshift clinic was humming with people. Matt wanted nothing more than to sit down and zone out for a bit.

He felt stirrings of homesickness for the first time in a few days. With a sigh, Matt tamped those feelings down. He just needed to get through the day. Maybe tomorrow would be different.

The new group filed in. Matt noticed one very pregnant woman sit near the back, wincing as she did so. She didn't look much older than he was. That thought bothered him and he pushed it – and her – out of his mind.

As he went through his presentation, he found his eyes going back to the pregnant woman. She kept shifting in her seat, small moans escaping her as she did.

A cold feeling began to seep into Matt. He found he was hurrying through the lesson, wanting to finish it sooner. Get her out of there. Before –

The woman uttered a piercing cry, clutching her belly. Matt forgot the lesson and ran over to her. "Are you okay?" he asked, immediately feeling stupid. Right, people who were okay started writhing and yelling in his presence all the time.

"The baby . . . " she panted. "It's coming!"

"Now?" Matt gulped. He saw everyone looking at him as if he knew what he was supposed to do. Who were they kidding?

The woman grabbed him by the hand. "Please, help me!" she begged. She cried out again.

Matt saw some from the Bible study looking his way. His mom caught his eye. "I need Dad!" he called to her. "Now!"

The Guyanese men and women who had been sitting in the class were standing, looking uncomfortable or confused. One woman came and sat next to the pregnant woman. "We should lay her down."

Matt shook his head. "Let's get her over to the doctors." He tried helping her to her feet, but she fell back with a wail. Her hand tightened on his and he winced. "Okay, let's help her lay down."

Matt and the other woman got the girl to lay down on the bench. She wouldn't let go of Matt's hand. He looked around frantically for someone to take charge. Where was his dad? What was taking so long?

The girl pulled her knees up, groaning in pain. The woman looked at Matt. "You need to help her."

He stared at her. "Lady, I'm not a doctor!"

She gestured firmly for Matt to sit where she was. "Come. I will hold her hand."

Feeling sick all over, Matt traded places with the woman. He glanced at the girl's long skirt, reluctant to touch her.

The pregnant woman let out a scream and that galvanized Matt into action. Blushing furiously, he lifted her skirt and was greeted with the top of a baby's head.

She hadn't been kidding. The baby was coming. *Right now*.

"It's coming," he croaked. What did he do? He thought about movies or television shows he'd seen when a woman was having a baby. "Um . . . I think she needs to push."

"That's right, son." To Matt's relief, his father was standing behind him. Matt hastily made room for his dad, who sat down, calm as anything. "All right, young woman, give me a push and you'll have a baby soon."

The young woman cried out, and Matt watched as his father pulled out the blood-covered baby, its eyes squeezed shut. As Matt watched, his father gently rubbed the baby's back and its pink mouth opened in a cry of protest.

"Congratulations, it's a boy," his father said. He quickly wrapped the baby in a clean towel that Gladys handed him and placed him in his mother's arms.

Matt was stunned. He'd never seen anything like this before. The new mother's face, covered in sweat, was alight with joy. "The baby . . . he is all right?"

"We need to check him out, but he looks fine at the moment," Matt's father said. He was doing something between the girl's legs and Matt looked away. He focused on the baby, amazed that someone could be so small.

The girl saw him watching and she smiled at him. "What is your name?"

"Me? Matt."

"Matt?" the girl frowned.

"It's short for Matthew," he explained. He felt shaky and he rested against the bench behind him.

The girl nodded. 'Matthew. A good name." She looked down at the baby, and her smile grew soft. "Matthew."

Matt blinked. Did she mean . . . she was naming the kid after him?

"Matt," his father said. "I need you to find Stan. We'll need someone to come out here and get her to a hospital. All right, son?"

"Yeah," Matt stammered. He noticed for the first time that everyone from the Bible study section was standing nearby, watching the whole thing. He scanned the faces for Stan but didn't see him.

Matt found Stan at the front check-in table. There was a long line of people waiting to come in while Stan and another team member handed out forms to be filled out.

"Stan," Matt panted, having run about looking for the man, "we need someone to come up here. We have a baby."

"What?" Stan asked, standing.

Matt explained as he led Stan back to where he'd been teaching first aid. The girl had her head in the one woman's lap, the one who'd ordered Matt about. The baby was snug in her arms.

Stan stood there, shaking his head. He pulled out a local cell phone he'd gotten from Steve Lockwood. "This has been . . . a very interesting mission trip." He dialed a number.

The older woman nodded at Matt. "You did a good job, young man."

"What?" Matt said. "I didn't do anything." *Except nearly have a panic attack.*

"You did exactly what you should do," his dad contradicted. He was cleaning his hands off with a reddened towel. "You got her comfortable, called for help, and were ready to deal with the situation if need be. You did fine, son."

Stan hung up the phone. "Steve and Anil are on their way." He looked at Matt. "It's going to take a while before you can resume the course. You might want to take a break."

Matt nodded. He couldn't resist a last peek at the tiny baby in his mother's arms before he left.

A little baby named Matthew.

- THIRTY-ONE -

Wow," ROBERT SAID, as Matt entered the break area. "That was amazing."

"I know," Matt said, sinking down into a chair. He shuddered. "I'm really glad Dad got there when he did."

"You looked totally competent," Robert said. "Like you knew what you were doing and everything."

Matt laughed. "Man, I was shaking like anything. All I could think was I was about to have a baby in my hands and I was scared I'd do something awful like drop him."

"You would've handled it," Robert said. He dug out a can of tuna fish and made a face. "Know what I hope when we get back? That your dad'll take us through some drive-thru. I miss a good cheeseburger."

"French fries with ketchup," Matt said with a nod.

"Onion rings."

"Spaghetti with a real meat sauce."

"Oh," Robert said. "You're right. Maybe it should be Olive Garden, not fast food."

Matt nodded as he pulled out his own canned lunch – macaroni and cheese this time. "I miss American food."

"I miss a lot of stuff," Robert admitted. "I wish I could've brought my dad's laptop. Then I could've talked to my family while we were here."

Matt took a drink of water. "You haven't heard from them at all?"

"Your dad's let me check my email," Robert said. "So we've swapped messages. But it's not the same, you know?"

"Yeah," Matt said. "I guess I'd miss my parents if they weren't here."

"You're lucky they're here," Robert said. "Hey, if they haven't gotten things cleaned up when we're done, want to sit in on a study or two? I bet Stan wouldn't mind."

"That'd be great," Matt said. "We can ask him."

Others trickled in, congratulating Matt on doing what needed to be done. He couldn't believe it. Didn't anyone realize how scared he'd been? He could've screwed it all up.

After their cold meal Matt and Robert sought Stan out. He was with the new mother, along with Gladys.

Matt noticed right away that his namesake was missing. "Where's the baby?" he asked Stan.

"Your dad's giving him a checkup," Stan told him. A grin quirked his lips. "Matt, I know you didn't want to teach the course, but don't you think making someone go into labor was a bit extreme?"

Matt felt his mouth drop open. Next to him, Robert was cracking up. A beat later Matt realized Stan was teasing him and had to grin back. "Well, it worked, didn't it?"

Now Stan was laughing. Gladys and the other women, who hadn't heard the exchange, shot curious looks in their direction.

When he was done, Stan, still smiling, shook his head. "All kidding aside, good job getting your dad out here and keeping people calm. I'm glad you were here."

Matt shrugged. "Gladys would've done better than me."

"Gladys was where she needed to be," Stan told him. "I believe you were too."

Before Matt could reply to that Steve Lockwood and Anil arrived. Lockwood glanced at the girl and then at Stan, Robert, and Matt. "The baby?"

"I'll check on him," Matt offered. At a nod from Stan he headed into the building. He asked one of the nurses in the triage section where his father was set up and was directed to a curtained off section in the back of the auditorium.

When Matt stuck his head in he saw his dad rewrapping little Matthew in a fresh towel. Someone had cleaned the baby up and Matt could see his face better.

"Anil and Steve Lockwood are here," he told his dad.

"All right," his dad said. "Do you think you could bring them the baby? That way I can start seeing patients again."

"Um . . . . " Matt felt a stab of fear. The baby looked so tiny and fragile, he was afraid he'd break him just by holding him too tightly.

His father lifted the child from the cloth-covered bench. He motioned for Matt to make a cradle of his arms. "Just support his head like this...put your other arm here...there."

Matt hardly dared to breathe. The child was so light. His little fists waved in the air, brushing Matt's chest with a feather-light touch.

"Let them know the baby appears to be in good health," his dad told him. "The hospital will want to check him out, no doubt. But he should be okay for the drive there."

Walking more carefully than he ever had in his life, Matt slowly made his way back to where the others waited. Several women who saw him smiled at the sight. He was sorely tempted to hand Matthew off to one of them but no one offered to take the child.

When he got back to Stan and the others, he was sweating – and not because of the heat. Steve and Anil turned to him, both focused on the baby in his arms.

"Well," Steve said. "I have to admit, in all the years People Helping People has been functioning, this is a first." He smiled at Matthew. "What did your dad say?"

Matt had to think a minute. "He said the baby was in good health and could go to the hospital,"

"Sounds good." He looked over at Anil. "Let's help the young lady to the car."

Anil took one final glance at the baby before following Steve. His eyes met Matt's. "Quite a miracle," he said softly.

Matt couldn't argue. He watched as Steve and Anil helped the new mother to her feet. She leaned on the two men heavily. Steve talked to her with a gentle tone, asking her name and other things as they walked.

When they came to Matt, the girl, who'd said her name was Evelyn, stopped. She smiled at Matt. "Thank you. Thank the doctor too, please."

The other woman, the one who'd helped Matt, followed after the men. She held her arms out for the baby and Matt handed him over, feeling a mixture of relief and sadness in doing so.

"I come back tomorrow," she told him. "You and I, we will speak, yes? You will be here?"

"Yeah," Matt said. "I'm Matt, by the way."

The woman smiled, showing a mouth of gaps in her teeth. "I am Helena," she said. "I will see you tomorrow."

With that she turned and followed the others out. Matt blew out a sigh of relief. He then looked at the mess on the bench.

Gladys followed his gaze. "We can get that cleaned up. You boys can give me a hand and we can start up the course again."

Stan nodded. "I think we can do that. Matt, if you can stick with it today, I'd appreciate it."

Robert spoke up. "Can I watch Matt do this? Then he and I can trade off doing Bible studies and teaching this course."

Matt turned and stared at Robert. "But you're good at the studies!"

"You'll be good too," Robert said. "I don't mind taking turns."

Stan looked from one to the other. "You two work it out. Gladys, I'll need you with the docs as soon as possible."

"Of course, Stan," Gladys said. She grinned at both boys. "All right, you two. Let's get to cleaning."

Some time scrubbing the bench and the concrete floor beneath it cleaned things up well enough that Gladys declared they could resume the first aid course. She insisted both boys use hand sanitizer on their hands after they cleaned things up. After commending them for their hard work, she left them to manage the course.

"So," Robert said, "what do we do?"

Matt saw people being waved to the benches. He lowered his voice. "Look, it's okay if you don't want to do this. I can handle it."

"It's no problem," Robert assured him. "I know you'd rather do Bible studies. I get that. If I can help you do that, it's a good thing."

Matt saw he couldn't win the argument. "Okay . . . well, thanks."

As he prepared to teach the first aid course, Matt suddenly recalled how many times he'd called his roommate "Righteous Robert" behind his back. And how many times Robert had reached out to him to give him a hand.

Matt was ashamed.

- THIRTY-TWO -

HOW ARE EVELYN AND THE BABY?" Matt asked Anil when the vans came to pick the team up.

Anil grinned. "They are well. The hospital was surprised to see them, I think, but they said that both mother and son were fine."

Matt breathed out a sigh of relief. "I'm glad."

Anil looked down the road, where several cows were slowly meandering towards them. "Evelyn told us she named the baby Matthew." He turned back to Matt, his eyes twinkling. "For the young American who was such a help."

Matt felt his face grow hot. "I really didn't do much. I'm really glad Dad showed up when he did – I was afraid I was going to have to catch the kid."

Anil smiled. "That is not what Helena said. She said you took charge and were a big help."

Matt shrugged. "Helena did as much as I did."

"You should stop doing that," Anil chided him.

"Doing what?"

"Minimizing your contributions," Anil said. "You may think you are being humble, but in reality you are not being honest."

Matt saw others of the team heading to the vans. "I dunno . . . Anil, I was scared silly the whole time. I just did what I had to, and I was afraid I was screwing it up."

"Being scared is normal," Anil told him. "You did not let it control you. Helena said others were there, standing around, doing nothing. You did something."

Matt shook his head. "You make it sound cooler then it was."

Anil grinned. "Believe me, it was cool."

On the way back to the hotel, Matt told Anil of his and Robert's plans to swap teaching the first aid course and doing Bible studies. "I'm nervous," he admitted. "What if I mess this up? I figured Robert would be helping me out, but this way I'm going to be on my own."

"You will not be on your own," Anil said, laying on his horn as he spoke. "God will be with you."

"But what if I tell someone something wrong?" Matt asked.

"I doubt you will do that. You know the gospel message, yes?"

"Well yeah, but . . . "

"But you know," Anil insisted. "Share that gospel message, and all will be well. That's all God expects of you."

"It's not that simple," Matt protested. "What if I –"

"These 'what ifs' are just Satan trying to discourage you," Anil said as he turned left. After almost two weeks it still looked like Anil was steering into oncoming traffic from Matt's perspective. "Concentrate on teaching the truth. You will surprise yourself with how well you do."

Matt wished he had Anil's confidence. "Easy for you to say. You're studying to be a gospel preacher."

"Yes, that is true," Anil said. "But you are a baptized believer, yes?"

"Yeah."

"You knew what the Bible had to say about salvation?"

"Sure. My dad studied with me before I was baptized."

Anil spread his hands, then quickly grabbed the wheel again as the van swerved. "What more do you need?"

Matt gave the driver a nervous look. "How about reaching the hotel in one piece?"

Anil laughed. "I am a good driver. And you will be a good Bible teacher. You will see! I will pray for you!"

"Okay," Matt said. Prayer couldn't hurt. He'd offer up a few of his own before tomorrow.

* * *

Matt hurried back to his room after the devotional, barely stopping to say good night to his parents. He found the notebook that contained the Bible study Robert had been using and, taking it to his cot, sat down and began to study it.

When Robert came to the room a short while later Matt was still reading the study with his Bible open next to him. "What're you doing?"

"Getting ready for tomorrow," Matt said as he tore a scrap of paper from his list of things to be thankful for. "I decided to bookmark the Bible verses – that way I'd find them quicker." He stuck the piece of paper into his Bible on the page that had Acts 2:38.

"Hey, that's a great idea," Robert said. "You probably won't need them after a bit, the Scriptures will be easy to find."

Matt frowned. "I feel so new at this. And I've been a Christian for several years."

Robert finished off his water bottle and reached for a full one. "At least you're doing something now. Lots of people never get around to sharing their faith."

Matt chewed his lip. "I just want to do it right."

"You will," Robert said. "Follow the study, share from your own life if you can find an application – and then, it's up to them."

Matt nodded. "Right. I'm just the watchman."

Robert grinned. "Exactly." He pulled off his shirt. "I'm gonna get ready for bed."

"Okay," Matt said, turning to another Bible verse the study indicated. "I'll finish up as fast as I can."

"No worries, your light won't keep me from sleeping," Robert yawned. "Take your time."

By the time Matt was ready to turn in, Robert was already snoring in his cot. He turned off his light and lay on his back, staring at the dark ceiling above him. *I'm really trying, God. Please, don't let me screw this up.*

* * *

Matt and Robert decided that Matt would start off with the first aid class and that they would switch places mid-afternoon. Robert would watch Matt teach the course one more time before the exchanged roles. "You sure you don't talk about how to deliver a baby in the class?" he asked Matt with a grin after the group had prayed for the day.

"Ha, ha," Matt said as they headed outside. "Just be prepared to scream for help if another pregnant woman shows up."

By the time Robert showed up to switch, Matt was feeling nervous all over again. He was tempted to tell his roommate that he'd changed his mind, he'd stick to the first aid course. At least he hadn't managed to mess that up, even if there had been some questions he couldn't answer.

"You eaten yet?" Robert asked.

Matt shook his head. He wasn't sure he could eat. He felt as if he were about to perform in a play – and he didn't know his lines.

Robert smiled and handed Matt the study notebook. "It'll be fine. I'll be praying for you."

Matt took the notebook and stammered out his thanks. He decided to go to the break area and catch his breath before he tried his hand at a solo study.

Matt found the break area crowded with several people, including his dad and Mr. and Mrs. Trask. He shifted from foot to foot, not really wanting company but not sure where else to go.

The Trasks left a few minutes later, and Matt sank down on the bench next to his father. His dad gave him a tired smile. "How's it going?"

Matt shrugged. "I'm getting ready to do some Bible studies."

"That sounds good," his dad said. "You okay? You seem a bit on edge."

Matt looked down at the cream-covered book, switching it from hand to hand. "I guess I'm really nervous about it. I mean, I want to try and do it, but . . . "

His dad gave him an understanding look. He put a hand on Matt's shoulder. "Want me to pray for you?"

Matt looked around. The others had left the small area and for the moment, he and his dad were alone. "Yeah. I mean, if you want to."

Both of them bowed their heads. "Father," Dr. Brooks said, "Thank You for all your many blessings. We've much to be thankful for on this trip. Please be with Matt as he shares Your message with others today. Give him the words he needs and let people see You and Your glory through him. In Jesus' name, amen."

"Amen," Matt repeated. He looked at his father, touched. "Thanks, Dad."

"You'll be fine," his dad said, giving Matt's shoulder a final squeeze before standing and stretching. "Well, time for me to get back to work. Let me know how it goes, all right?"

"Sure," Matt said.

To his relief, he found he was less nervous then he had been when he came in. Taking it as a good sign, Matt dug in his backpack for a can of hot dogs and beans.

Maybe he wouldn't stink at this after all.

— THIRTY THREE —

N O," THE YOUNG MAN SAID. "I cannot be baptized."

Matt tamped down the frustration that welled in him. "You understand what the Bible teaches, right, Phillip?"

"Yes, I do," Phillip said. He ran a hand over his close-cropped curly hair. "But my family, they are Hindu. I cannot change my faith."

"But you said you agreed with what the Bible taught," Matt reminded him.

"Yes, yes," Phillip nodded.

"Then shouldn't you do what it says?" Matt asked.

"I cannot do it," Phillip said, shaking his head. "Maybe some other time."

Matt looked around. Others were sitting, like him, conducting Bible studies. He saw Harry talking with a young woman that Mrs. Trask was apparently studying with. They looked quite serious.

Matt sighed. He couldn't interrupt Harry to ask for help, and everybody else appeared to be busy at the moment. "You do realize that later might not happen, right?" he asked, making one more attempt.

"Yes," Phillip said. "I will think about it maybe later."

Inwardly Matt groaned. "Okay, let me sign your sheet and then you can go see the doctor."

"Yes, thank you."

Matt watched as Phillip took his sheet up to Stan, who was directing people on where to go. Rocking his chair back on two legs, Matt took a long drink of water and thought about how the afternoon was going.

He'd done three studies, two women and Phillip. Each person had listened to him attentively, nodding as he made point after point. Each of them had been polite.

Each had said no.

Matt didn't understand how they could agree with everything he said and then not act on it. He wondered if he were the problem, if he was just not being clear.

Because strait is the gate, and narrow is the way, which leadeth unto life, and few there be that find it.

Matt recalled the verse in Matthew. It didn't make him feel any better. He dropped his chair back onto its four legs and leaned down to pick up his Bible. Maybe he should just swap back with Robert after all . . .

"Hello, Matthew."

Matt jerked his head up to see an older Guyanese woman standing in front of him. Her graying hair was pulled back into a bun. She wore a faded floral print dress and sandals.

He recognized her from yesterday. "Oh, hi . . . ." He struggled to remember her name.

She handed him her intake sheet. "Helena," she said. "We met yesterday, remember?"

He glanced down at the sheet, feeling his cheeks heat up. "Yeah, I do. Sorry for not remembering your name."

She waved his apology aside. "You see many people, yes? It is all right."

"Well, um, have a seat," Matt said, and the two of them sat on the hard folding chairs. "How's the mom with the baby?"

"I see her today. She is well. The baby is well."

"Good," Matt said.

"I would have come sooner, but I went to see her," Helena said. "I wanted to talk to you."

"Okay," Matt said. "Well, that's good. Um, thanks for helping out yesterday."

She smiled at him. "You did well. Evelyn was grateful. If the doctor had not come, you would have handled things."

"Yeah, well, I 'm glad the doctor came," Matt said with a nervous laugh. He looked down at her intake sheet and saw that she'd left religious affiliation blank. "Um, do you go to church?"

"No," Helena said with a shake of her head. "When I was a child, yes, I went. But when I got older . . . it did not seem important."

Matt opened up the study notebook. "Well, you believe in God, right?"

"Yes, yes, I believe in God," Helena answered. "Are you going to talk about God?"

"Yeah," Matt said, wishing he wasn't so nervous again. The other studies had shaken his confidence. "Wait, you said you wanted to talk to me about something?"

Helena cocked her head. "You believe in God?"

"Yeah."

"And in Jesus? You are a Christian?"

"Yeah, I am."

Helena nodded. "I have not heard about Jesus in a long time. I do not read the Bible, I do not go to church."

Matt looked down at the laminated pages. He heard drops of rain plunking on the roof and looked up to see it starting to pour outside the covered area. Jenna and the others working with the kids came running for cover, laughing as they did so.

"Do you believe that the Bible is God's word?" he asked Helena.

"The word of God. Yes," Helena said, "I think I do believe that."

Using the study to guide him, Matt talked about the Bible for a few minutes. Helena nodded throughout his explanation and appeared to agree with his points.

Matt swallowed. "Okay, well, let's see what the Bible has to say about us – and our relationship to Him."

He spent several minutes laying out the gospel message. Man had a problem – he was sinful and separated from God because of his sins. The only hope he had was for someone to pay the price that sin demanded.

"Jesus was the only person who could pay that price," Matt said. "He never sinned, he lived a perfect life here on Earth."

Helena nodded. "Yes, yes."

Matt hesitated. He wiped the sweat off his face. "You have any questions so far?"

"No, no," Helena said. "I understand."

"Okay," Matt said. He talked about how Jesus rose from the dead, and thus had given man the opportunity to have a relationship with God.

"I know Jesus rose from the dead," Helena said. "I remember that from when I used to go to church."

"Great," Matt said. "Let's talk about how we respond to this gospel message."

Matt talked about the plan of salvation – how a person became a Christian. He spoke about how a person had to hear the message and believe in it. Then they had to confess Jesus, repent of their sins, and be baptized.

"Baptized," Helena said. "I have to go into the water?"

"Yeah," Matt said.

Her hands went up to pat her hair. "I have to get all wet?"

Matt nodded. "It's part of becoming a Christian," he said. "Were you ever baptized?"

"No, no," Helena said. "I seen other people get baptized, when I was little? But I have never been baptized."

"It's not too late," Matt said. "You could be baptized today – right now – and all your sins would be washed away."

"Yes, yes," Helena said. "I have many, many sins. I have not lived the way the Bible teaches. I know this."

"That doesn't matter," Matt said. "God forgives all sins, if you give Him a chance."

Helena studied her clasped hands for a long moment. Matt glanced down at his Bible, wondering what else he could say to persuade her. She seemed on the verge of deciding.

"What if I sin after?" Helena asked. "I do not think I can be perfect."

"No one is perfect," Matt assured her. "I goof up all the time, but then I pray to God to forgive me. He understands we won't be perfect."

"You still sin?"

"Yeah," Matt said. "I try not to, but sometimes it's hard."

"It is hard, yes," Helena said. "I lived with a man, I did not marry him. He died last year. I have three children. They do not know Jesus. I would like them to."

"I get it," Matt said. "But you need to know Jesus as well. There's no reason you can't become a Christian now, is there?"

"I do not know," Helena said. "It is something I need to think about."

"What do you have to think about?" Matt asked.

"I do not know," she sighed. "It is a big decision."

"It is a big decision," Matt said. "The most important decision you'll ever make. That's why I want to help you. How can I help?"

Helena's gaze wandered outside, where the rain still poured. Matt prayed to himself. *What else can I say, God? What else can I do?*

"What will my children say?" Helena's voice was soft, as if she wasn't talking to Matt. "Will they understand?"

"Helena," Matt said. The older woman looked at him. "I understand your worry. When I got baptized, I worried a little about what my friends would think. But I decided I had to do this. It's the only way to have a relationship with God. If my friends didn't get that – well, it didn't make it any less right."

"Yes, yes," Helena said. "You are right."

"You don't have to say yes today," Matt said. He realized that he suddenly didn't care if he got someone baptized or not – he just wanted to help this woman who was struggling with a decision. "God doesn't promise us tomorrow, though. You know what you need to do now. It's up to you."

Helena studied her hands. Matt saw Harry straighten up from talking with someone and waved the preacher over.

"This is Harry," Matt told Helena. "He preaches here. Maybe he can help you."

Harry crouched down in front of Helena and took her hands in his. "What is the problem?"

"I am worried about my children," Helena said. "They do not know Jesus. What if they do not understand? I have no other family."

"If they do not understand, they do not understand," Harry said. "But you will not be without a family. You will have God's family. We are together brothers and sisters."

"Do you really think your kids won't get it?" Matt asked. "That they won't love you anymore if you become a Christian?"

Helena thought about it. "I think . . . they will still love me, yes."

"We will help you tell them about Jesus," Harry assured her. "You will not be alone."

Matt found he was holding his breath. He wished he could talk to Helena's kids, help her explain things to them.

"Do you know what you need to do?" Harry asked.

"Yes, Matthew explained it to me," Helena said.

"Then will you do it?"

Helena was silent a long moment. Matt silently said a prayer for her, that God would speak to her somehow.

Finally, Helena nodded. "Yes, yes. I will do it. I will become a Christian."

- THIRTY-FOUR -

MATT COULDN'T STOP GRINNING. "That's great!" he said. Impulsively he hugged Helena. "That's great," he repeated.

Helena hugged him back. "I knew yesterday I needed to talk with you, Matthew. I needed to learn about God from you."

Harry was smiling. He stood and gestured to two Guyanese women who were standing by the door to the auditorium. "These sisters will give you clothes to change into so you can be baptized."

Helena started to go with the women but hesitated. She looked at Matt. "You will be there? You will baptize me?"

"Me?" Matt said. Helena nodded and he turned to Harry. "I've never baptized anyone before."

"It is not difficult," Harry said. "I will explain to you while we wait."

Matt swallowed. "Okay. Sure."

Helena smiled at him. "Thank you, Matthew."

Harry threw an arm around Matt's shoulders. "Come on. Let's get ready. The rain is letting up, so you won't get too wet."

Matt's hands were shaking a little. He let Harry lead him to the edge of the enclosure. Sure enough, the rain was tapering off, leaving everything steamy and humid.

Matt didn't care. He listened as Harry explained what he needed to say and do. It was simple, but Matt was glad for the instruction. Harry led him to the barrel full of water they were using for a baptistry.

People were gathering around to witness the baptism. This made Matt nervous. But he was excited as well. He was helping someone become a child of God. He found he couldn't keep the smile off his face.

He caught his mother's eye as she joined the group. She smiled at him and mouthed the words, "I'm proud of you." He ducked his head, but his smile remained.

Before he knew it Helena was standing in front of him, dressed in the faded shorts and t-shirt provided for her to be immersed in. Matt and Harry helped the older woman up the stepladder and into the barrel.

Matt spoke to Helena in low tones, explaining what was about to happen and what she needed to do. She nodded in understanding. He then raised his voice. "This is Helena Dharminda. She has studied God's word and is ready to become a Christian. Helena, what is your confession?"

"Jesus is Lord," she said, her voice soft but firm.

Matt's own soul soared at her words. "Helena, because of your confession, I'm able to baptize you in the name of the Father, of the Son, and of the Holy Spirit."

Helena pinched her nose shut. Matt took her wrist in one hand and laid the other on the back of her neck as he gently lowered her into the water.

Once she was fully immersed, he pulled her back up. There was a chorus of "Amen!" from the group, and someone started to sing, "God is So Good." Others chimed in, Matt included, as he and Harry helped Helena out of the barrel.

She was trembling but smiling through tears that coursed down her face. "I am not apart from God anymore," she said, hugging Matt.

He hugged her back, not caring that his clothes were getting wet. "That's right," he answered.

Harry led the group in a prayer, thanking God for Helena and praying for her to continue in the faith she'd found. He also prayed that God would work on her children's hearts, that they also might come to know Jesus.

Matt silently thanked God as well, grateful for Helena and her choice. He prayed others would also hear the message, even if it wasn't from him.

The group began to break up. Harry shook Matt's hand. "You did well. Keep up the good work."

"Thanks," Matt said. "I appreciate you helping me out. I wasn't sure she was going to say yes at the end."

"God's word spoke to her through you," Harry said. "That is what made the difference. I just followed what you started."

Before Matt could say anything else his mom came up and embraced him. "Honey, this is fantastic! I can't wait to let your father know."

Matt let his mom hug him for a moment. "Thanks Mom, but I just did what you've been doing all along." He pulled away, and suddenly remembered his previous attitude. "I hope it makes up for the way I've been acting."

"You've been doing better," his mother encouraged him. "I know you're trying. I think God knows as well and is rewarding your efforts."

"Look!" one of the women said, pointing at the sky.

Matt looked up to see a brilliant rainbow arcing in the sky. He stared at it for a long moment, just enjoying it.

Yes, it was hot. Yes, he was tired. Yes, he was even a little homesick. But for the moment, he was glad he was in Guyana.

* * *

Matt couldn't wait to tell Anil about Helena and her baptism after the clinic shut down for the day. Anil clapped him on the back. "See?" the Guyanese man said, "I told you there was nothing to worry about. I prayed for you, and God answered my prayers."

Matt's grin dimmed, but just a little. "No one else I studied with decided to become a Christian."

"But one did," Anil reminded him. "And you delivered the message. You were the watchman. Now their souls are in their own hands."

Matt couldn't argue with Anil. And his good mood was so powerful even those who'd rejected the gospel message couldn't dent it very badly.

Robert spoke to him while they were moving benches out for the gospel meeting. "I heard someone you studied with became a Christian today. I knew you could do it."

Matt grinned as they placed the bench down on the hard concrete floor. "I can hardly believe it. It was so exciting."

Robert smiled back. "It's great when God uses us to do His will."

"Yeah," Matt said. He remembered how often he'd mocked Robert's lifestyle behind the teen's back. He was suddenly uncomfortable, guilt piercing his good mood.

Matt sat quietly during the gospel meeting, warring with himself. He'd done something good – scratch that, something great. He could turn around and see Helena sitting in the back, along with Barry's mom. Barry caught his eye and giggled.

Matt turned back to face Harry, who was speaking that evening. He tried to listen to the message, but his mind kept wandering back to the cruel things he'd said about Robert.

What would Jesus do? Well, Jesus wouldn't have said those things in the first place, Matt knew that much. So perhaps the better question was, what did Jesus want Matt to do?

One answer kept coming back, and Matt couldn't say he was very fond of it.

Before he knew it, the gospel meeting was over. Matt was kept busy moving benches back out of the way for the final clinic day that would take place tomorrow.

He got to Anil's van in record time. Soon they were driving back to the hotel. Matt said little on the trip, too busy wrestling with his thoughts to engage in conversation.

Anil said nothing about Matt's mood shift until they returned to the hotel. As people emptied out of the van Anil leaned against Matt's door, keeping him in the van. "You are not as happy as you were."

Matt decided to come clean. "Can I ask you something?"

"Of course."

"What if . . . what if you'd been making fun of someone but they didn't know about it?" Matt asked. "What if you suddenly realized you were wrong about them?"

Anil rested his head on his hand, still leaning on the van door. "I suspect you know the answer to the question."

Matt sighed. "I guess. I don't think I like it, though."

"Sometimes doing what is right is not pleasant," Anil said. He straightened up and opened Matt's door. "But it is better to do it then not to. And you will feel better afterwards."

Matt got out of the van, feeling a weight on his shoulders. "I guess you're right."

"May I offer some advice?" Anil said. "The sooner you deal with this, the sooner it will be off your heart. The Lord said to leave your gift at the altar and reconcile with your brother if necessary. It is a good command."

"Right," Matt said. He looked at the brightly lit hotel. Robert was in there somewhere. "Thanks, Anil."

"I will pray for you, Matt," Anil said. "Do not forget that God is still with you, even in this."

Matt said good night and walked into the hotel. He saw a few people heading for the dining room for their late dinner. He stuck his head into the large room and saw that Robert wasn't there yet.

Matt decided to check their room. He caught Robert locking their door. "Hey, Robert? You have a minute?"

The other teen frowned. "Sure, but we don't have long, you know."

"This shouldn't take long," Matt said, trying not to gulp. Robert narrowed his eyes but unlocked the door and went into their room, Matt following.

Once in the room, Robert turned to face Matt. "Okay. What's up?"

Matt let his gaze travel around the room, suddenly unable to meet Robert's eyes. "Well, it's just that . . . you see . . . um . . . "

"What?"

Matt swallowed. This was so much harder than he'd expected. "It's just that . . . I think I owe you an apology."

Robert said nothing, and Matt forced himself to look at the other teen. Robert looked a little wary, but didn't seem inclined to help Matt out.

"You see . . ." Matt continued. "I've said some things about you...I was just kidding, you know? But I realize now . . . well, it wasn't really cool of me to do that. And I'm sorry."

The other teen's mouth twisted. "You think I didn't know about it?"

Matt felt his cheeks burn. "I . . . I guess I thought you didn't."

Robert snorted. "Trust me. You weren't always as quiet as you thought. 'Righteous Robert' and all that? Yeah, I know. You aren't the first to make fun of me, Matt, and you won't be the last."

"But you never said anything."

"What good would it have done?" Robert said. "To be honest, I almost asked for another room – I figured you were gonna make the time here miserable for me."

Matt's gaze dropped down to the floor. "Yeah, I kinda felt the same way."

"Shows what we know," Robert said. "You're not the jerk I thought you were, Matt. I'm glad we got to know each other."

"So . . . you're not mad?" Matt looked up again to see a faint frown on Robert's lips.

"Well, I am a little," Robert admitted. "But I'll get over it. Now come on, I'm hungry and I don't want to miss dinner."

"Yeah," Matt said. He started for the door and then jumped when Robert punched him in the arm. "Ow!"

"Sorry," Robert said. "I meant that to be a friendly tap."

Matt rubbed the sore part of his arm. "Sure."

The boys eyed each other for a few seconds, then started laughing.

"I *am* sorry," Robert said as they headed out the door. "I guess I was madder than I thought."

"It's okay," Matt chuckled. "I think I deserved it."

Feeling good about things with Robert, he followed his friend down to dinner.

- THIRTY-FIVE -

MATT WOKE UP THE NEXT MORNING with mixed feelings. On the one hand, he still felt good about the day before. And they would be heading home the next day, back to the United States and all he missed there.

But that meant that this was the last day here in Guyana. To his surprise, that thought bothered him to a certain extent.

Robert was still snoring on his cot when Matt went into the bathroom. He was still asleep when Matt got out of the bathroom, showered and dressed for the day.

Grinning, Matt grabbed his pillow and flung it at his roommate's head. "Rise and shine!"

Robert groaned something unintelligible and tossed the pillow back at Matt. "What was that for?"

"I woke up first," Matt said. "Come on, it's time to get up."

Robert dragged his phone off his nightstand and checked the time. "You're right," he said. "Okay, I'm up. Gonna wait on me for breakfast?"

"Sure," Matt said. He held up his own phone. "You've got ten minutes."

"Funny," Robert growled. He grabbed his clothes and headed for the bathroom.

Matt flopped back on his cot to wait. He picked up his own phone and began to scroll through some of the pictures he'd taken over the two weeks. Laughing kids. The Kaieteur Falls. Jenna.

Jenna. Matt sighed. He was glad he and Robert were now friends, but it felt like he hadn't gotten anywhere with Jenna over the two weeks. He still felt tongue-tied around her.

And he couldn't forget what he'd heard her say about him in the stairwell that night. Granted, things were very different now. But still . . .

Robert came out of the bathroom, scrubbing a towel through his damp hair. "You going back to bed already?"

"Nah," Matt said, swinging into a sitting position. "Just thinking."

Robert glanced at Matt's phone and Matt realized that he still had the picture of Jenna on the screen. He jabbed at the Home button on his phone and the photo winked out.

Robert grinned. "You like her."

Matt thought about denying it, but what would be the point? He settled for a shrug. "Doesn't matter. She doesn't like me."

Robert frowned. "What makes you say that?"

"Well . . ." Matt heard his stomach rumble. "Hey, I'm starved. Let's go eat."

Robert studied him for a minute, and Matt was afraid he was going to push the conversation. Instead, he shrugged. "Yeah, food sounds good. Let's go."

* * *

Anil was in his usual good mood when Matt headed for his van. "Ah, your last trip to the clinic! It will be a good day, yes?"

"I hope so," Matt said as he took his customary seat in front.

Anil shut the door for him and leaned into the open window. "You seem peaceful. You took my advice?"

Matt glanced over to where Robert was talking to Dr. Lopez and his wife. He gave Anil a nod. "Yeah, I did. Everything's cool."

"See? God is wise. He tells us how to fix things and when we do as He says we are blessed."

Matt grinned. "I guess you're right."

Anil laughed. "Of course I am right." He slapped Matt's door. "I will miss you, Matt. I cannot say that about everyone who passes through here."

"I'm gonna miss you too, Anil," Matt said, knowing it was true as he said it. He frowned as he thought. "You don't have a computer, or we could talk sometimes."

Anil's eyes brightened. "Ah, but we can. When I am working for Steve, there is a computer in the office. He has that program, what is it called, Skype? Where you can speak to someone online?"

"Yeah," Matt said. "But would he be okay with that?"

Anil's eyes twinkled. "We can ask him. We can also write to one another. I will give you my address, and you give yours to me."

"Sounds good," Matt said. "I'll get it to you before we take off tomorrow. Are you driving us to the airport?"

Anil nodded. He saw that the van was filled and he slammed the side door shut. Once he was in the driver's seat he said, "Yes, we will be here at two AM. You will be awake?"

Matt grimaced. They would be catching an early morning flight back to the United States. Because they had to load up everything and also be at the airport two hours early, they would have to leave the hotel in the middle of the night.

"I'll be awake," he told Anil. "Sort of."

The drive to the site seemed to go quickly for Matt. Before he knew it they were at the church building. Matt hopped out and hurried to help get ready for the patients that would be coming this last day.

He saw Jenna already with a few children of those Guyanese women who were helping out at the site. He spotted Barry with the kids and decided to say hi.

Barry grinned and ran up to Matt as he headed over. "Matt!" he called. He then changed his expression to an exaggerated frown.

Matt grinned. He poked Barry in the ribs. "You think I can't get a smile out of you?" he chuckled.

It didn't take long before Barry and several children who'd gathered around Matt were all laughing. Matt couldn't help but laugh as well. He felt a small tug on his heart as he snapped pictures of the kids. Some more people he was going to miss.

Jenna came over, a small toddler in her arms. "You going to be working with us today, Matt?"

He had been crouched down at the kids' level when she came up. Now he stood, feeling his nerves hit him full force. "Uh, no. I'm gonna be doing the first aid talk and some Bible studies."

She nodded. "I heard someone you studied with got baptized. That's really great."

"Yeah," Matt said. He looked down at the kids surrounding him, all trying to peek at his phone. "Well, I'd better go see if I need to do anything."

"Sure," Jenna said. "Come on, guys, let's play some Duck, Duck, Goose."

Matt watched as Jenna led the kids away to where Susie was waiting. He sighed, remembering Robert asking him why he thought Jenna didn't like him.

His relationship with Jenna was a dark spot on the trip. Matt really liked her, and he wished he could find a way to talk with her without his tongue getting tied up in his mouth.

As he turned away from the kids and Jenna, Matt pushed those thoughts aside. Today was his last chance to make a difference in Guyana. He needed to have his head in the game.

* * *

". . . Thank you for the opportunity to be here. In Jesus' name, Amen," said Stan.

"Amen," Matt echoed, along with the rest of the congregation. He opened his eyes.

People bustled around, gathering up children and chatting with one another. Darkness was falling outside and the lighting in the building was poor. Matt spoke to one of the teenage boys who'd sat in front of him. A sharp poke in his shoulder made him turn around.

A man he didn't recognize stood in front of him. Helena stood a little behind him, her expression apprehensive. The man's dark eyes bored into Matt. "You are Matthew?"

"Yeah," Matt said. He wondered what was going on. The man wore a stained tan dress shirt and khakis, and was a head taller than Matt.

"You studied the Bible with my mother?" the man demanded, jerking his thumb back towards Helena, who flinched.

"Yeah, I did," Matt said. He suddenly wished his dad or another adult would come up to speak with him, to help him with this conversation.

The man's eyes narrowed. "Why? Why tell my mother she needs Jesus? You want her money, is that it?"

"What? No!" Matt protested. "I didn't take any money from her. I was just sharing the Bible with her."

The man snorted. "Christians. You talk all holy but you just are schemers. You want something from her, I know it."

"That's not true," Matt said. "All I did was share the good news with her. We just want for her to have a relationship with God. I swear it."

The man frowned. "You are American. You will leave here. Then what?"

To Matt's relief Harry came to stand beside him. "Is there a problem here?"

The man pointed at Matt. "This American talked my mother into becoming a Christian. She hasn't needed God before now. What do you want from her?"

Harry shook his head. "We are demanding nothing from Helena. You have nothing to fear, Lawrence. We take nothing from you."

Lawrence scowled. "I must look after my mother's best interests. You know that."

"I do," Harry agreed. "But this young man did nothing wrong."

"I can show you what I showed your mom," Matt offered. "Then you can see for yourself we didn't do anything to hurt her."

Lawrence's eyes narrowed as he studied Matt. "You would do this? Right now?"

Matt nodded. He knew he might get in trouble – they were supposed to be finishing breaking down things and getting back to the hotel – but he couldn't leave things the way they were.

Harry touched his arm. "Matt has to prepare to leave. But I can show you what he taught Helena. It is nothing secret."

Lawrence looked from Harry to Matt. He turned to Helena abruptly. "You wish this?" he asked.

She trembled but nodded. "I chose this. They did not force me. I would live for Jesus now."

"Fine," Lawrence said, throwing up his hands. "Then so be it!" He stormed out, leaving people staring at him as he passed by.

Harry shook his head. "Lawrence is very protective. Too much so."

Helena twisted her hands. "I am sorry for this, Harry. And Matthew. He does not wish me to be a Christian. He does not understand."

Matt shrugged. "It's okay. What are you going to do?"

"I am going to do what the Bible teaches," Helena said. "It will be hard though. You will pray for me?"

"Of course," Matt said.

Harry put a hand on Helena's arm. "I will pray as well. When Lawrence calms down, perhaps he will be willing to listen to me. You call me if you need anything."

"Thank you," she said.

During the exchange, Matt's parents came up. "What was that about?" Matt's dad asked, looking from Matt to Harry. "Is everything all right?"

"It is fine," Harry assured them. "Helena's son disagrees with her decision to obey the gospel."

"So he came to yell at Matt?" Matt's mother asked. She looked at him. "Are you all right?"

"I'm fine," Matt said. He looked at Helena. "It's fine," he repeated. "Are you going to be okay?"

Helena nodded. "Thank you, Matthew. I will be fine. I thank you for everything you have done. May God bless you on your trip home."

"Thanks," Matt said. He looked at his parents and Harry. "I guess I'd better give a hand in putting stuff up."

"Go ahead," Harry said. "Thank you for what you have done, Matthew. You have changed much in the time you have been here, it is a good thing."

Matt felt his cheeks heat up. "Thanks," he repeated.

As he headed to where others were loading up the vans, Matt thought about what Harry had said. The Guyanese preacher was right – he *had* changed.

So where did he go from here?

- THIRTY-SIX -

ROBERT CAME UP TO MATT after the devotional on the roof of the Phoenix. "So, you going to try to catch some shut-eye?"

Matt folded a chair and carried it to where they were being stacked. "Naw. I mean, what's the point? I'd have to get up in about four hours."

"I hear you," Robert said. "Some of us are going to play some board games that Chuck brought. You want to join us?"

Matt thought about it as he and Robert walked over to get some more chairs. "I guess." He paused as he caught sight of Jenna, talking to her parents near the edge of the roof.

Robert followed his gaze. "I don't know if anyone's asked Jenna. Why don't you?"

"Um," Matt said. He was suddenly interested in the chair he was folding.

"Come on, man. She likes you, you know," Robert said.

Matt's head jerked up. "No, she doesn't."

"Yeah, she does. She told me so," Robert argued.

Matt shook his head. "She thinks I'm a jerk," he said. "I heard her talking to you last week."

Robert rolled his eyes. "That was last week. She's not blind, she sees how you've changed. You need to give her some credit."

Matt dragged his chair to add to the stack. "I don't know."

"Look," Robert said. "Go ask her. Worse thing she says is no. She's not gonna push you off the roof or anything."

· "Okay," Matt said. "Just to shut you up."

Robert grinned. "Works for me. We'll be outside by the pool. See you there."

Matt nodded and walked slowly towards where the Trasks stood. He waited until Jenna hugged her parents and they left before speaking up. "Uh, Jenna?"

She turned towards him. "Yes?"

"Well," Matt said, dropping his gaze to his feet, "some of us are going to stay up and play games for a bit, and I wondered if you wanted to come."

Jenna said nothing for a moment. "Is that what you're going to do?"

"Well, I guess so," Matt said. "I'm not going to bed, are you?"

"I'm not tired," Jenna said. "I guess we can play games for a bit, if that's what you want to do."

"Well," Matt said, "is there something else you want to do?"

Jenna shrugged. "I just thought we could talk a little."

"Talk?" Matt asked.

"Yeah," Jenna said. Her gaze dropped down to her scuffed sneakers. "I mean, we don't, really. I'd like to just get to know you."

"Okay," Matt said. He wondered if he'd be able to form words during this talk. He looked around nervously. Most of the team had already left the roof. "Um, you wanna go downstairs?"

Jenna agreed. Together they headed for the door and down a flight of stairs. They were quiet while they waited with a few others for the elevator and traveled down to the lobby.

When they went back outside, Matt took a deep breath of the warm humid air. He saw Robert with a group of fellow young people. Several board games were stacked on a table nearby.

"Hey Matt, you guys playing?" Robert asked.

"Not right now," Matt said. He saw Jenna drift towards the pool. He swallowed the urge to pull Robert aside and ask the other teen for advice. "Maybe later, okay?"

"Sure, no problem," Robert grinned. He picked up one of the board games and turned towards Chuck. "How about Risk?"

Matt followed Jenna to the pool. She dropped into a chair near the water and he sat down next to her. Looking at the shimmering surface he racked his brains for something to talk about.

Jenna broke the silence. "What's your favorite Bible verse?"

He jumped slightly. Frantically Matt tried to come up with an answer, but his mind was blank. "I guess I never thought about it," he admitted. "What's yours?"

"Romans 8:28," she answered. "You know which one that is?"

Matt thought about it for a moment. "And we know that all things work together for good to them that love God, to them who are the called according to His purpose," he quoted.

She smiled. "That's right."

"Why is it your favorite?" Matt asked.

"Because of what it promises," she said. "No matter what happens, God can make some good come from it. Even bad things."

"Yeah," Matt agreed. "Like coming here – I thought this would be totally awful, you know? That I'd hate it every minute I was here."

"But you changed," Jenna said.

"I guess I did," Matt admitted. He flushed a little, remembering the first few days in Guyana. "I wasn't really that great of a person at first, was I?"

Now Jenna's gaze moved to the pool's water in front of them. "Well . . . you had an attitude. It kind of surprised me."

"I didn't want to come," Matt said. "My folks made me. I swore I'd sulk the whole trip."

"I'm glad you didn't," Jenna said. "It would have ruined the trip."

"Yeah, I guess so."

A small silence fell between them. Matt heard laughter from the table where Robert and others were playing Risk.

"Be right back," he told Jenna. He got up and went to the table where the games were stacked.

A quick search came up with a deck of cards and a checker board. He grabbed both and brought them both back to where Jenna sat. He showed them to her. "You want to play cards or checkers?"

* * *

"Seriously?" Matt laughed. "I haven't even read the books."

Jenna ducked her head as she jumped one of his black checkers. "I guess *Twilight* is more for girls than boys."

Matt grinned. "Sparkling vampires? Really?" he looked down at the board in front of him and his grin faded. "You didn't tell me you were such a good checkers player."

"You didn't ask," Jenna replied. She played with some of his captured checkers. "What about the *Pirates* movies?"

"Yeah, I liked those," Matt said as he pushed one of his checkers forward. "Johnny Depp totally rocks."

The game had helped the two of them break the ice. Matt found that having something to do, something to pay attention to made him feel less awkward around Jenna.

The two of them had dragged a table by the pool to set up their game. Other than telling the larger group of players to keep the noise down, the staff had pretty much left them all alone.

Matt drained his water bottle. "Hang on. I gotta get a refill." He went to a table where the staff had left some bottles of distilled water. He took two and brought one back to Jenna.

"Thanks," she said. "I was about out."

Matt studied the clear plastic bottle. "It's gonna be weird not having to brush my teeth with bottled water anymore."

Jenna giggled. "You're funny."

Matt looked at her with a raised eyebrow. "Do you mean funny-strange or funny-haha?"

She laughed. "I meant it in a good way. Whichever way is better."

Matt grinned. "Okay. Then, thanks, I think."

They continued to talk and play checkers, not looking at the time. Finally Chuck and Robert came to where they were sitting.

"Hey guys, sorry to bother you but it's one-thirty and I want to get stuff packed up."

Matt pouted. "But I'm winning!"

Jenna laughed. "Okay, so we'll say you won this one. That's still three for me and two for you."

Matt made a face as he and Jenna slid the checkers into the box. "One more game and I would've had it tied up. I was figuring you out."

"Sure, sure," Robert said. "Quit being a crybaby."

"I'm not crying!" Matt protested, then shook his head at Robert's grin. "Okay, okay. Here, Chuck, thanks for letting us use it."

Chuck took the checkers game and cards. "Thanks guys. See you in a few."

"I'll help you load this stuff up," Robert said as he followed Chuck to the table where the games were stacked.

His prop gone, Matt felt his old shyness steal back. "So . . . you have any other packing to do?"

Jenna nodded. "My mom and dad are probably up by now . . . I should go help them."

"Sounds good," Matt said. He stood when Jenna did and together they walked back inside the hotel.

It was very quiet as they made their way to the Trask's room. Both of them felt the need to lower their voices, aware of the number of people sleeping behind the closed doors.

When they got to Jenna's room, she paused. "Matt . . . "

"Yeah?" He thought he could hear her parents moving around in the room.

She fiddled with her room key, not looking at him. "When we get back home . . . will you still talk to me?"

Matt couldn't speak for a moment. He swallowed and said, "Uh, yeah. I mean . . .if you want me to."

She looked up at him and smiled. "I do."

"Okay then," Matt said. "Um, I guess I'll see you in a few minutes."

"Yeah, I better get inside," Jenna said. "I enjoyed playing checkers with you."

"Yeah, me too," Matt said. "I'll talk to you later, okay?"

"Okay," she said, still smiling. Matt waited until she went into her room before heading to his own.

He had to work at keeping quiet. He really wanted to run and shout, but he knew that no one would thank him for waking up half the hotel. He settled for hurrying down one flight of stairs and hurrying to his room.

Robert was already there, stuffing some clothes into his suitcase. He looked up when Matt came in and grinned. "Well? Was I right?"

"Shut up," Matt muttered, but he couldn't keep the smile off his face.

"I told you!" Robert crowed. He continued in a sing-song voice. "She likes you. You like her . . . "

Matt snatched his pillow off his bed and threw it at his roommate. "You'd better not give her a hard time about it!"

Robert dropped a shirt he was holding and caught the soft missile. "I'll behave, I promise. But I gotta have a little fun with you!"

Shaking his head, Matt muttered, "I can't believe I thought you were a goody-goody."

His pillow came flying back at him. "Told you I wasn't perfect!" Robert laughed.

The pillow hit Matt in the side of his head. He caught it before it tumbled to the floor. "Truce! Okay? I still gotta get ready."

"Better hurry," Robert said, glancing at his watch. "If we're not down there by two, Steve Lockwood will have a fit."

Matt nodded and went to grab his stuff from the bathroom. He couldn't believe that he'd be gone from this place in a few hours.

And how mixed his feelings were.

- THIRTY-SEVEN -

Mᴀᴛᴛ ᴀɴᴅ Rᴏʙᴇʀᴛ hauled down their suitcases and backpacks to join the group of mission workers in front of the Phoenix Hotel. The boys were among the last to come down. Steve Lockwood was already outside, directing the packing of the luggage.

"Guess we should help," Robert said, as they surveyed the controlled chaos.

Matt nodded. There was an air of unreality about everything. Aside from their group, no one else was outside. People spoke in hushed voices, mindful of sleeping folks in the dark hotel. Matt stifled a yawn as he followed Robert to where the suitcases were piled and looked around for instructions.

"Matt Brooks!" Steve Lockwood zeroed in on him. "Come over here a minute!"

What have I done now? Matt thought. He glanced at Robert, who shrugged as he grabbed the handle of one of the large black suitcases and began to roll it to a waiting van.

Matt walked over to where Lockwood stood. The bearded man finished giving Anil some instructions and then turned to Matt.

"Once we get to the airport, I'm going to be busy getting you all going. I wanted to talk with you before then."

"Okay," Matt said. He wasn't trying to be snotty, but he was tired and worried that in spite of everything, Steve Lockwood still had it in for him.

Lockwood folded his arms and shook his head. "I'm not going to lie to you, kid – after that first day I wasn't sure you were going to make it here. I figured I was going to have to have you babysat the whole two weeks – and I wasn't looking forward to it."

Matt thought about Monday, almost two weeks ago, and suddenly couldn't meet the older man's gaze. "Yeah. I didn't have that great of an attitude, I guess."

"You don't have to guess. You didn't," Steve said. "I watched you for a while. I was sure you'd blow up again, do something stupid, really wreck the work here. But your folks and Anil went to bat for you. 'Give him a chance' they said."

"My parents talked to you?" Matt hadn't known that.

"Yeah. Not just them. Stan Conner pled your case, and your roommate put in a good word for you too. They all said you were basically a decent kid and you'd come through in the end. Well," Steve sighed and smiled. "In the end, they were right and I was wrong. I'm glad you were part of the team, Matt. You helped make it a successful trip."

Matt blinked. "Um . . . thanks, I guess."

Steve extended his hand and Matt shook it. "I hope you'll return next year with the group. I know Anil will be glad to see you again. So will I."

Matt nodded. "Okay. Thanks for telling me that, sir."

"You're welcome. Now let's get moving here, we want to get you all to the airport on time!" Steve said, clapping his hands. Matt took the cue and headed back to the pile of luggage, while his brain turned over what Lockwood had said.

* * *

Once the luggage was loaded, people moved to the vans. Anil waved Matt to his van. "One last time, we ride together!"

Matt grinned as he climbed into the front seat. "I'm not gonna see driving in the States the same way, Anil. Thanks to you."

"I am a good driver!" Anil insisted with a broad smile. "You will learn to drive soon, yes?"

"Yeah," Matt said, buckling his seatbelt. "If my parents let me."

Anil shrugged. "You are a responsible young man. I believe they will permit it."

Matt gave the young Guyanese man a tired smile. "Maybe you can put in a good word for me. Like you did with Steve Lockwood."

Anil glanced out his window before pulling into the street. Their van was second in line in the caravan. "I only told Steve the truth. Your actions proved me correct."

Matt leaned his head back on the seat. His body seemed to be reminding him that it was after two in the morning. "How did you know? I mean, I didn't exactly have a great attitude when you first met me."

"This is true," Anil said with a laugh. "I was quite angry with you when we first met. But do you know what told me you could change?"

Matt was glad that the noise of the van gave the two of them a little privacy in their conversations. "What?"

"You admitted that you had . . . how did you put it? Ah, yes! You said what you'd said about hating Guyana was stupid. You did not try to defend it." Anil slowed down to make a wide right turn, then grinned over at Matt. "Even though you were still quite an angry young man, I saw that you were not totally lost. You just needed some time. And some help."

"Well, you were a big help," Matt said. "I probably wouldn't have gotten through the past two weeks without you."

Anil shook his head. "It was not me. It was God. He worked in your heart, in your mind. He is the one who should get the glory."

Matt smiled. "Okay, God gets the credit, but He used you to make it happen. And a lot of other people too."

"Yes, yes," Anil agreed. "He does use us in His work. I am glad to have met you, Matt, and I hope you will write to me."

"Sure thing," Matt said. He pulled out a piece of paper with his home address written on it. "You write to me, too, okay?"

"Yes, okay," Anil said. "We will become great pen pals!"

Matt nodded and lay his head back against the seat once again. He heard the murmur of conversations behind him. The windows of the van were open, and he smelled odors that reminded him of a trip to a farm – manure, and animals. He decided to close his eyes, just for a moment . . .

He jerked upright as Anil stopped the van. "Whoa. Did I fall asleep?" Matt asked as he rubbed at his eyes.

Anil grinned. "You snore! I did not think the drive was that boring!"

Matt groaned. "Sorry about that. I guess I was really tired."

Anil waved away Matt's apology. "It is all right. You did not get any sleep tonight, yes? So it is no wonder that you are tired."

Matt looked out the window. He recognized the airport. Anil quickly got out of the van and opened up the side door for the passengers.

Matt climbed out of the van. He stretched and then grabbed his backpack from the front seat. Going around to the back of the van, he helped Anil unload the suitcases that were stacked there.

Before too long several of the drivers appeared with handcarts. Luggage was piled up onto these and the carts were carefully steered towards the airport entrance. Matt walked alongside the one Anil pushed, a hand on the luggage to keep it from tumbling.

The airport was well lit and the long process of checking things in began. Matt was kept busy hauling suitcases to their owners so they could be properly processed. A line formed in front of the airline counter as weary mission team members pulled out their passports and checked that their suitcases were properly labeled.

Finally, Matt tracked down his suitcase and one of the black bags that Stan asked him to check with his stuff. Anil was standing to the side, watching him. The young Guyanese man waved at Matt.

Matt walked over to where Anil stood and stuck out his hand. "Thanks again for everything."

Shaking his head, Anil pulled Matt into a hug. "Love you, brother. Safe travels back home."

Embarrassed, Matt returned the hug briefly before pulling away. "I gotta go, I guess."

As Matt turned to leave, Anil spoke one last time. "Hey Matt, you come back next year, yes?"

Matt stopped. He thought about Guyana, with its bugs and heat. Having to brush your teeth with bottled water. The hard, sweaty work.

He thought of little Barry, with his young friends. The Kitaurer Falls. Helena and the joy on her face when she'd come up out of the water. The talks with Anil.

With a huge grin he turned back to his friend. "Count on it."

And with that, he headed over to stand in line to go home.

For now.

About the Author:

LAURA WARE has traveled to Guyana, South America several times, twice on medical mission trips. Her column "Laura's Look" appears weekly in the News Sun (Highlands County). She has written several novels as well as short stories. Laura lives in Central Florida. Check out her website at www. laurahware.com

www.ingramcontent.com/pod-product-compliance
Lightning Source LLC
Chambersburg PA
CBHW031029260626
47153CB00016B/1010